The Group: Aaron

JL Foulk

Writing as

Jenn Amato

Jenn Amato

Find me on the web
https://www.jennamatoauthor.net

<u>Don't forget to sign up for my spam-free newsletter</u>
https://bit.ly/3HLMA4g

AngryEaglePublishing.com

Dedication

This book is dedicated to Jeff Thomson, Dan Uebel, Jack Childress, Angel Ramon, DJ Cooper, and James Dean. Without you psychos, I wouldn't be here. My cheerleaders and biggest fans, I love you crazy bastards to the moon and back. You're my chosen family and I couldn't ask for a better group of nuts. I also want to thank Angry Eagle Publishing, LLC for believing in me and continuing this journey.

Contents

From The Group: Stacy

Aaron, of course, went with the boys. Jana stayed behind. We located a spot behind a mom-and-pop grocery store and secured the empty campers and cars. Freya was staying in the RV that she and Dan shared so that one didn't need to be secured. We gathered around as the boys piled in the single truck and camper. Jason felt that we needed to leave his attached to give the illusion that they were traveling, and they were it. Dan and Freya said their goodbyes just in case it was the last time they saw each other. Sadly, we have to think about those kinds of things even more now. When we leave each other or split the group, there is a good chance people may not come back. This is life as we knew it...and it is FAR from fair.

Jenn Amato

1.

I crouched quietly in the dark, the light that was outlining the door bright and flashing as cops ran by. The cops were right outside looking for me. They found the car and thought they were looking for a person in their late teens, not a child who just turned eleven and could barely reach the pedals. I was small for my age and ate like the proud owner of a bottomless pit. My foster parents put a lock on the fridge and the cupboards in the house so I could only eat when they deemed it appropriate. I loathed Keith and Dawn. They only wanted me there so they could collect a check. Being small had its advantages. I was able to hide in the smallest places, where the officers wouldn't think to look for me. Right now, I am hiding in a cupboard in an abandoned house in the north end of Toledo. Not just any cupboard, a cupboard at eye level to the officers.

'They always check the lower cabinets but never the upper ones.' Just as that thought passed, I heard a scraping on the door like the person on the other side

was grabbing for the handle of the door I was sitting behind. I began to sweat as the scraping intensified and was beginning to sound otherworldly. My eleven-year-old brain couldn't comprehend what could be making the noise. No longer did it sound like whoever was out there was grabbing at the handle. It sounded as if someone, or something, was digging at the door. The worst part about all this was I couldn't see anything. It was pitch black in there. The light that outlined the door had recently gone dim and seemed to be going darker, offering no indication of where the door was any longer.

The scratching, correction, DIGGING, on the door seemed to have stopped and now I didn't want to breathe. Trying to hold my breath in my little lungs proved to be a futile attempt to protect myself as the door started opening and all I saw was a faint light as if the room were being lit by the full moon. The door, slowly opening wider, showed a dark silhouette of a person. I let the pent-up air out of my lungs and put my little hands up as if to say "You got me". The silhouette just stood there continuing to open the door, the room behind them lit by the moon. A sudden breeze of chilly air made my small body shiver. I didn't remember it being this cold. Where was my coat?

The door to the cupboard I was hiding in finally opened all the way giving me a little bit of light so I could see part of the one standing in front of me. It was...*Dawn?* No, it wasn't Dawn. At least it didn't look like Dawn. Dawn, as mean as she was, had beautiful mid-length hair and smooth skin. She didn't look like this...monster...that stood before me. The thing in front of me resembled her, had her eyes but her face was...falling off. She had flaps of skin hanging, stuff oozing from her eyes and nose, and if I didn't know any better, her teeth were razor sharp and oddly long, protruding from her mouth a bit. I was having a hard time registering what I was looking at until it spoke. "Aaron." I just looked at it, my head cocked and confused.

"Aaron," the thing in front of me said louder, its arm raising as if to slap me as Dawn used to, right in the face. My voice caught in my throat. I wasn't even sure I was breathing. The arm got higher and the flesh fell off the bone like a well done roast in the crockpot.

I noticed at the end of her fingers were nails that looked like claws or talons. The nails were jagged and sharp looking with pieces of the last clawed meal stuck in them.

"AARON!!!" screamed the thing in front of me in an unrecognizable, almost demon-like growling voice as she swiped to slash my face with those nasty nails of hers.

I jolted awake at the nightmare. '*Oh shit! Thank God it was just a dream.*' Jason noticed I had jumped a bit in the back of the crew cab truck as Dan, Jason, and I made our way down the main road into town. We were waiting for a sign from the mystery radio man, Nick. I could see that Jason and Stacy were kind of in the middle of a tiff when the rest of us were walking up to meet them before we decided for us to go.

"You good?" Jason asked, looking at me in the rearview mirror.

"Yeah. Bad dream," I answered as I stretched and rubbed my eyes. Two of my worst fears wrapped up in one nasty dream. That bitch Dawn and her being a zombie. Fucking horrible.

I hadn't thought of her since I was removed from her home. She and that piece of shit husband of hers, Keith, beat me so bad I was in the hospital for a week when I was twelve. My crime, you ask. I was twelve and a boy. I got caught stealing porno magazines from an adult bookstore that was right around the corner from our house on Lagrange and Detroit. Man, they hated me.

The radio squawked to life, "That there is far enough, Yank. We will be there to get ya. Just y'all stay put." It was Nick in all his country glory. Why did he call Jason "Yank", though? We weren't that much more north of this area. Jason slowed to a stop, put the truck in park, and took the keys out of the ignition. He tossed them in the center console cup holder and radioed to Nick that he had done so. Also told him if he wanted to check, there would be a shotgun in one of the closets in the camper. I felt this was giving him too much info but I had learned over time that Jason did everything for a reason. It was one of the many things I admired about him. It also made him popular with the ladies and that was something I wanted, too.

Nick and a couple of his big-for-nothin', corn-fed goons went through the camper while a young lady with some of the nicest tits I ever saw watched us, shotgun in hand and pointed at us, ready to pull the trigger if necessary. She wasn't playin' about keeping the men safe that were rummaging through our camper, but even serious, she was beautiful. Things were tingling and I didn't want to give it away.

Nick came back out, "Yeah, I found yer shotgun. I'm kinda sorry about this, but you can never be too careful nowadays."

Jason smiled at him and responded with his usual, "No worries." Like it wasn't a big deal. Here I am feeling violated and it wasn't even my stuff. I came a long way from being the punk kid that would have tried to fight these country bumpkins. I always had a little knife on me because the streets taught me that I needed to always have one. Can't trust anyone. Until the day I met Jana and Stacy after I crashed my stolen car into a street lamp pole. I immediately trusted them and I'm sure I pissed them off because, in all honesty, I was still a little jerk who knew nothing.

"Let me welcome you to McComb. We ain't got much but we are happy to share what we got. If ya act like a fool, Jeb here to my left will kindly see you out." The thin old man, Nick, bobbed his head over to the huge younger man who looked like he could eat a whole village and still have room for dessert. My eyes went wide because of course his name was Jeb. Why would it not be? Had he not been as big as a semi-truck, I may have laughed. It left me wondering what the guy on the right's name was. He looked like Jeb, just a bit smaller.

Jason spoke for us, "That would be great. We appreciate it, sir. We will earn our keep for the time we are here and I can promise you, we will be very respectful of you and your family. What would you like us to do now that we got those pleasantries out of the way?" I am rolling my eyes on the inside. Why are we even doing this?

The lesser big boy piped up, "Just follow me. I'll be driving in a black Ford dually." Now that made me snort out loud. His big, shaved head turned and looked at me, and I instantly lost the giggles.

"You got a problem, city boy?" the meathead asked. He then spat tobacco juice at my feet, thankfully missing but still made me sick.

"I'm sorry. Allergies," I lied through my teeth. I didn't want to get flattened like a pancake on my first day with these people. Jason gave me a look that made me shoot a glance at the ground in shame.

We piled back into the truck to follow Big Boy to wherever their compound was. I was beginning to regret coming along. At least I would have had some freedom with the girls. I can't believe we left them without a male. I'm not a pig, I do think women are capable but, in this world...there are no rules.

2.

Robert was driving the long way around Bowling Green to see how bad the city was. No one at the camp knew he was gone. They didn't know where he was headed, which may not have been smart. If the shit hit the fan, Robert was stuck fighting on his own. He took the best truck on the compound to make sure he wouldn't have any mechanical problems and John was standing at the truck he would have taken. Robert was slowly coming out of his embarrassed rage but when he left, he did not want to take John with him. He needed to breathe.

On his travels, he happened upon a few campers that he thought had people in them. If he had had time, Robert would have hooked them up and hauled them to a survivor camp nearby. Since he didn't, he found some zombies, led them over to the campsites, and let the zombies loose. They should be zombie food right now. That thought made him giggle.

He was driving down State Route 65 going to the Bowling Green chapter house. He didn't know the exact address but he knew the house was across from the hospital. These people had wanted a front-row seat to the end. Angie and Rick were in charge of the chapter but hadn't been heard from in months. Robert thought he would check on them to find out why since he had all sorts of pent-up rage coming to a slow simmer during his drive. He also wanted to have more information for his father so maybe he wouldn't think Robert was a screw-up after he told him how Saginaw went.

Robert pulled into the driveway of the chapter house, slowly. It was a long driveway as the house was situated on a bigger plot of land across the street from the Boon Hospital in Wood County. He kept the truck running and just sat there looking into the open attached three-car garage. No sign of zombies and no sign of life. Robert shut the truck off and began to carefully walk up to the garage. When he got into the garage, he grabbed a shovel. He left his gun in the truck because he didn't want to attract more zombies if he had to kill any.

Robert listened at the door and heard Rick and

Angie but couldn't make out the words they were saying. Robert stood there just listening, trying to make out what they were saying, to no avail. Robert tried the door handle and found it unlocked. He slowly opened the door and quietly closed it in case he needed to surprise someone. The Toledo chapter had tried getting a hold of these people and they didn't respond to any attempts. There was no reason for them not to respond, they were alive and well. So, what had they been doing?

Robert came from the hallway that led from the garage into the kitchen. He could hear Rick and Angie loud and clear now. Robert could hear a third person whimpering and muffled screaming.

"I need more tape around her mouth. She's too loud," Rick could be heard saying from the kitchen. He had to be in the living room since he wasn't immediately in view. Was Angie whimpering?

"I'm working on it. Just give me a minute. Her hands are coming loose." That was Angie. So, she's ok...now who is the third person? Robert came around the corner, shovel still in hand, from the kitchen to the dining room. He slithered along the wall to keep from being seen. As he got closer, the third-person whimpers were getting louder.

Robert got to the corner leading into the living room and snuck a peek, just allowing his head to clear the corner for a visual. There was Rick, butt-ass naked, with some poor girl strung up in the middle of the living room. Her arms were being held up by some rigged contraption bolted into the ceiling, positioned slightly forward and her feet secured to the floor, spread slightly more than shoulder width apart with her middle resting on a sawhorse, making the naked female's rear end pop out. Rick was balls deep in this lady, sweat dripping down his back. Angie was also naked, running around with her old ass vagina out, making Robert want to puke. He thought the roast beef jokes were just that. Here it was, they were true. A shiver went down Robert's spine. On closer inspection, the woman that was strung up was no longer human and was not whimpering. She was growling. Robert could get over Rick stringing up a woman but this woman wasn't even a woman. She was a zombie! She had a bite on her left arm, on the inside by the elbow. Robert almost puked.

Having seen enough, Robert stepped around the corner he was hiding behind and said their names.

"Rick, Angie, what the fuck is going on? My father and the organization have been trying to contact you…we thought you were dead, man."

Angie and Rick turned around to face Robert in their birthday suits. The look of shock and surprise on their faces! Angie tried to explain while grabbing a robe she had laid on the couch. Rick pulled out of the zombie lady and turned towards Robert with his one-eyed monster looking at him as if he were next. Robert did not doubt that Rick had fucked dudes in his lifetime.

"We found her lurking around the house and wanted to teach her a lesson. During the lesson, she turned. Rick said she was still good so we kept going. She hasn't fully turned yet…" Angie stammered through her explanation to Robert while Rick looked on, hands on his hips and visibly going soft.

"Angie, we have been trying to fucking call you

over the ham. You guys are in here playing slap and tickle with a fucking zombie? That's gross, for one. Two, your area has been handed over to the Toledo chapter because you haven't responded. We thought you were dead." Robert held the shovel to his side and saw Rick eyeing it up.

"Like hell, you have our sector," Rick retorted. "You can't do that to us, you miserable little pissant!"

Robert started feeling his rage come back to life. This sick fuck was trying to tell him what was up. "You better calm your man tits there, pal. You have no recourse. The Federation made its decision. Now go get dressed and let's get up to our camp. The Fulton County chapter now has three areas to look over and because of your little...activities....here, you need to be tested. Get your ass in line and you better have a good excuse for not responding to The Federation OR my father!"

On that note, Angie and Rick went to get dressed. Robert looked closer at the woman hanging from the contraption bolted to the ceiling. She was turned; all the way turned. Now he just needed to figure out how he was gonna get Angie and Rick back to camp without them turning. He would make them ride in the bed of the truck. That would keep them from biting him. If they turned on the way, he would figure out how to dump them.

'This is exactly what I was hoping to avoid,' Robert said to himself as he was looking around the house trying to find the radio. Finally, the two idiots came out to the living room dressed and carrying bags of clothes.

"We're ready, Robert," Rick said, not even looking at him.

"Do you guys have any weapons in the house?" Robert asked, going over to the spot where he had leaned the shovel against the wall. He wanted to grab it before they got any bright ideas.

"No. We used all the ammo to take over this place. That lady is the neighbor and none of the rich bitches out here believe in weapons. It's a college town," Rick answered.

Robert nodded his head slowly, giving Angie and Rick the belief that he understood. "Well," Robert said, getting a better grip on the shovel. "I guess I should be on my way," Robert said as he wound up. Using the shovel like a baseball bat, he swung, smacking first Rick and then Angie in the head. The sound was similar to hitting a gong. They both went down hard. They weren't knocked out, just dazed from getting hit.

Robert ripped the tape from the zombie lady's mouth, then released her strung-up arms so she could have dinner thanks to her captors. Robert got away from the newly freed zombie and watched her, from afar, start chewing on Rick's shoulder. He started yelling and that sent the zombie bitch into a feeding frenzy, eating more and more of his arm down to his wrist. Angie was screaming now because Rick was getting eaten basically on top of her. He was too heavy to move. The zombie lady ate at Rick's arm quickly and while she was chewing, Rick turned.

Angie, still screaming, was scrambling to get out from under him, and Rick, the newly made zombie, just turned his head, and bit right into Angie's flabby, pancake tits. He ate those till she turned. Robert guessed it maybe took a total of thirty minutes for all this to occur. It felt that long but he couldn't be too sure as he did not have a watch or a way to tell time. He didn't have to clean up all the blood because no one would be coming to investigate.

Robert, while walking out to his truck, thought about how all the world was about before the virus was time. Everything revolved around time before but now, he made the rules. Robert climbed into his truck and began the trek back home. He had something to go back to and tell his father about. He could honestly say that the leaders were dead. Dear old Dad didn't need to know he killed them unless he asked. Robert did feel better now. He was able to work out his frustrations with those two who were ignoring the radio calls from his camp. They should have never been put in charge but they didn't have many options.

The ride back for Robert was very quiet. He contemplated staying at that beautiful house to get some shut-eye but he decided he wanted to sleep in his bed. He had been up over twenty-four hours and figured another thirty minutes wasn't gonna hurt. He even made record time back to the camp. Without traffic, it was quick!

Robert noticed that there were small groups of survivors traveling during the early morning hours, trying to use the sunlight and good weather. Robert heard about a central location for survivors but at that moment, couldn't recall where it was. That was probably because of the lack of sleep. A few people walked out into the street to try to flag him down but he just kept going, laughing at the people he left behind in the rear-view mirror. He would deal with these survivors later when the crew came out to build a survivor tank.

Robert decided to drop in on the group running the Lucas County chapter of the Ohio Federation. His family was now in charge of Lucas County, Fulton County, and Wood County. Since he was out, he figured he would stop and see how John and Peggy were doing. They were living in the old Ford mansion in the Old West End subdivision in Toledo and were the first to implement Operation Infect. They carried the virus to one of the biggest hospitals in the city, St. Mary's. It went off without a hitch and people started infecting the non-infected at an impressive rate. John and Peggy were seen as heroes by The Federation. It was, after all, their daughter, Connie, who devised the infection from two viruses.

She was as close to a scientist as The Federation could get, she was the best crystal meth cook in Lucas County. Naturally, The Federation picked her to find the correct combination of viruses to create this nasty one that would spread like wildfire. Connie was able to find the right mix of viruses and an ingenious delivery system. Robert was impressed by her and was hoping to see her when he checked in on them. He was not only impressed, but smitten.

John and Peggy weren't much to be impressed with. They were good friends to Robert's parents. That's the only reason they got the position they were in. William and Tina were the ones in charge of the three counties and William put John and Peggy in charge of Lucas County. Once his father figured out who he would appoint to the newly acquired Wood County area, Robert decided to shoot his shot with Connie. He had fantasized about having her more than once and he knew he liked her because he had always treated her with respect in his daydreams while jerking off.

Robert was almost at their home. He loved that they picked the village within the city of Toledo, Ottawa Hills. This was where all the wealthy people of Toledo lived. He even knew there were a few actors that had taken up residence in the village a while before the infection took hold. This meant that the house was super big. Bigger than the one in Bowling Green that the losers took over. Robert had formed a little crooked smile just from thinking about the way the two died by his hand. The people in Ottawa Hills were so spoiled that the police department had keys to their homes, the officers would walk their dogs and even take the residents' trash to the curb. The level of service that the police department provided for those people in the village was astonishing. To be fair, the police department didn't have much to do.

Robert turned from West Bancroft Street onto Talmadge Road, then drove just a few seconds north till he got to John and Peggy's street, Westchester Road. Robert located the house that they took over once the world turned topsy-turvy and pulled into the drive that was almost like a street of its own. The garage alone was bigger than the studio apartment he had before the world flipped on end. Robert shut off the truck, looked at himself in the rear-view mirror to make sure he didn't have anything on his face, and proceeded to get out of the truck and walk up to the front door, smoothing out his shirt on the way. His palms were sweating.

KNOCK, KNOCK, KNOCK. Robert took a half step back so they could see who was coming to the house. He also knocked extra loud so that no matter where they were in the house, they could hear him. He wasn't sure about the electrical situation. 'Do doorbells run on electricity?' he thought to himself while waiting for the door to be answered. It was probably a stupid question, but he couldn't help it. He needed to distract himself so he wasn't thinking about "her".

The front door was pulled open and when Robert looked up, he almost choked on his spit. Standing before him was Connie, the object of his fascination. She looked beautiful as ever even if she was only dressed in an oversized button-down shirt.

"Hi, Robert. What brings you by?" she asked as the smile on her face widened.

"I was in the neighborhood so I thought I would stop by and see how things are going with you. May I come in?" Robert even surprised himself with his manners.

"Well, of course!" She stepped aside just enough so that Robert could squeeze through but would still end up rubbing his chest and arm on her perky breasts. You could tell she never had kids. Them puppies were solid. Robert stuck his hands in his pants pockets to try to hide his erection.

John came into the foyer. "ROBERT!" he yelled excitedly, as if there weren't monsters outside that could be awakened from their stationary slumber by noise to eat their faces.

"Hello, Sir. I was just stopping in to check on you and see if there was anything you needed. "The two shook hands and John escorted Robert to the great room as they chatted. They talked about the plan, the meeting up in Saginaw, and the approval of The

Federation with the plan execution. Then he discussed with John how he found Rick and Angie in Bowling Green.

The Rick and Angie story was a lie of course. No one could know that he killed them by making them turn and leaving them there. Robert couldn't help but notice as the men were talking that Connie was sitting in a recliner, one foot under her, the other swung over across her tucked leg and the arm of the chair. She still only had on that damned button-down shirt which didn't help Robert get rid of his erection. The white, stained button-down shirt was also not buttoned up. Connie maybe had three of the middle buttons secured which allowed him a pretty nice visual of her breasts but not the nipple. Those could be seen through the white shirt. Was this for him or was she always this seductive?

Jenn Amato

3.

Nick's group pulled up to his farm and we followed them. The giant boys of his pulled their trucks up to a pole barn a few feet from the house. The two big guys got out and directed us where to park at the side of the pole barn while Nick was already parked and out of his vehicle closer to the house. Jason, Dan, and I jumped out of the truck. We walked up to meet up with Nick as the boys and that pretty girl followed us.

Some fair-skinned older lady around Nick's age came out. She walked up to Nick and kissed him then asked him what was going on while side-eyeing us.

"This here is Jason, Aaron, and Dan, honey. We happened upon each other over the radio and decided to meet them. They looked alright so I thought they could come back with us. They aren't staying long. Boys, this is my wife, Jennifer. Don't let her fool ya, she's meaner than a rabid raccoon."

Jason politely waited for Nick to finish. "Hi, Ma'am. I'm Jason. We will be leaving in the morning. We are just looking forward to talking to people who aren't trying to kill us. We have run into some nasty people out there."

Jennifer smiled at us, put her hand out for us to shake, and said, "Don't you believe him. I'm only mean to him when he deserves it. Come on in. I have some stew on the stove that you boys are welcome to."

We followed the family into the house. My mind started wandering again as to what the girls were doing. Why did we leave them behind is going to forever linger in my mind. As we walked through the door from the side of the house into their little mud room, Jennifer stopped and pulled a gun from her waistband, and pointed it right between Jason's eyes.

"OK, stop right there. Nick and the boys are gonna strip you down once Bella and I leave the room to check you for bites. No offense, I hope you understand. While Nick may think you're ok out there, I have total control in here. No arguing, please. Just comply so we can all have dinner." Jennifer put her gun back in her waistband and turned to walk through the door to go into the kitchen beyond. She closed the door behind her and Jason let out the breath he was holding.

Nick looked at Jason with a smirk. "Better get to it. My little lady don't play."

We all stripped down to our skivvies as the girls left and went inside. Nick and the boys looked over every inch of us. I felt like I was back in jail. No bites were found and we were able to get dressed. We followed the family into their home. There we were, standing in the kitchen chatting, surrounded by the two huge, giant brothers who we later found out were twins. Jebidiah and Josiah. They weren't even related to Nick and Jennifer. They had been around the family so long that they just melted into it when their parents didn't make it in the first wave of infection. Nick and Jennifer took them in as if they had always been a part of the family. I wish I had that when I was left alone. Now, as for the beautiful, gun-toting brunette, I found out through chatting that her name was Bella and she was Nick and Jennifer's daughter; a fresh nineteen-year-old daughter. The perfect age for me and let me tell you, I am in post-apocalyptic love.

"Well, everyone, I made a good dinner once I heard Nick was bringing back survivors. We haven't seen many and some we have seen have been less than nice. We took care of them and buried them in the backyard. They made the mistake of assuming we were some country bumpkins." Jennifer stated matter-of-factly as she was getting all the food on the table. This woman scared me.

Jason's eyes went wide and met my equally wide eyes, which also met Dan's even wider eyes. We were all thinking it, did she just say they buried them in the backyard? We looked over at Nick who just wore a huge smile on his face like he was proud of his wife.

We all sat down at the table and had the best home-cooked meal of our lives. I felt a bit guilty that the girls were missing this. How long is Jason going to make us stay?

As I pondered the question, Jason spoke up, "So, we just wanted to make sure that we could pass through. We have a couple of vehicles that we didn't want to lose in a fight if you guys weren't friendly. That's why we came. We wanted to show you that all we wanted to do was pass through town. We weren't expecting all this."

"Well, Jason, we would be happy to escort you out of town down State Route 186. We know that there is a family down the way that isn't friendly. They won't mess with us though, so we will get you past them. Then you can be on your way," Nick said to Jason.

Dinner was done, I helped clear the table with Bella, because it gave me a chance to talk to her. She wasn't biting. None of my usual bad-boy antics worked with this girl. She was less than impressed. This was my last chance at scoring with a cute chick and I struck out.

"Aaron," Jennifer said to me, "you don't have a chance with Bella. She is a Daddy's girl and her boy toy is her Springfield XDM 9mm I gave her for her birthday this year. You can't hold a candle to that firepower, son."

Everyone stopped what they were doing and just looked at me. The twins straightened and stood stoic as if they needed to defend their little sister's honor. The damn woman couldn't just pull me aside and say anything. She had to embarrass me in front of everyone. All I could do was smile stupidly and say, "I don't know what you mean, ma'am."

"Uh-huh," Jennifer said with a smirk. Bella was blushing.

We finished cleaning up and told Nick we would radio him when we got close to town tomorrow. Jason told him we would meet him in the same spot as we did today. Nick shook everyone's hands, as did the twins. We made our way back to the girls and that's when my anxiety was at an all-time high. Were we going to go back and find our stuff ruined? Were we going to find everything okay? Are the girls going to be in pieces or part of the walking dead?

"What did you think of them?" Jason said, cutting into silence.

"I liked them," Dan said. Dan honestly liked everyone. He didn't see a bad trait in anyone he came across.

"I liked them. Even if Jennifer did embarrass the hell out of me at the end." I said, chuckling, which got everyone chuckling. Then it was the Aaron roast hour.

"Well, you were very transparent," Dan said.

"I had to shoot my shot. Who knows when I will see a fine piece of ass like that so close to my age," I retorted.

We got back to where the girls were waiting and Stacy came out of the travel trailer that all the girls were huddled in.

"We didn't expect you guys back till tomorrow. How were they?" Stacy asked Jason.

"They were great. They are going to escort us through the city. They said there is a family that they know to be unfriendly, but are afraid of them. And Jennifer, the matriarch, said that the family won't mess with us if they see us escorted by them. So, tomorrow, we will meet them in town and they will send us off safely."

Freya and Dan hugged. Freya looked at Jason and asked, "How bad is that family?"

I answered, "We don't know. We never asked. We were just grateful they were going to get us through the town." I yawned. I was exhausted now that I was back with our people. I didn't realize how long I was on high alert.

We went to bed in our respective cabins. The night was dreamless for me, thankfully. I didn't need another visit from Dreadful Dawn in my sleep where I am supposed to be safe. The morning was a different story.

"FIRE!"

That's what I heard when I was startled awake right as the sun broke the horizon. That's when I smelled it. A mix of wood, electrical, rubber, and something odd permeated the area where I was sleeping. Then I began choking.

"SHIT! My trailer is on fire!" I jumped out of bed, surveying the situation I found myself in. What I was able to see was a huge fire in the front and middle of the trailer. I was stuck in the rear of the trailer in the bedroom. I dropped to the ground on my hands and knees after realizing the smoke was at my eye level. Thankfully, this was a newer model and had windows in the back bedrooms that doubled as emergency exits. I crawled over to the window and opened it. I tumbled out, completing a somersault but landing on my back in the gravel. Dan and Freya saw me and yelled to Jason, Jana, and Stacy that I was out on this side. It looked like they were trying to detach the 5th wheel from the truck that I used to haul it.

Dan and Freya helped me up off the ground and Jana came over to check on me.

"Oh my goddess, are you ok?" Jana said in her posh British accent. I could hear her talk all day.

"Yeah, I'm ok," I said as I swatted at my clothing trying to get off the dirt and rocks but also putting out any fire that may have tried to ignite my clothing. "What the hell happened?"

"We don't know. I was making breakfast for Dan and I smelled wood and plastic burning. I saw smoke float by my window so I looked and saw your trailer on fire. Did you leave anything on?" Freya said as she also checked me over with Jana.

"No, I was knocked out. It was the first night I was able to get some good sleep without nightmares." I stopped slapping myself, satisfied that I was not on fire and looked over at the trailer in amazement. We had no way to put it out so it was going to have to just burn itself out.

"We better back away from it. There is propane on the front of that and when it's time to blow, it will be a spectacle," Dan said. He walked over to Jason and Stacy to see how they were doing getting the trailer dislocated from the truck. Sadly, the truck melted into the trailer and there was no saving it. The three of them started backing up as they saw something the rest of us didn't.

"We need to get a move on. This puppy is about to blow at some point. I can see the flames licking the truck's fuel tank and propane tanks like it was pleasuring a mistress," Jason so eloquently stated it as a long-winded way to say *"She's gonna blow"*.

I jumped in with Stacy, and everyone else started up their rigs and began to move away from the ticking time bomb. I was once again without anything that identified me as even just a human. I had just the clothes on my back, just like when I was a kid. The gravity of that fact, added to the immeasurable amount of stress we have had over the last few months, was too much for me to handle anymore and I broke. Sitting in the passenger seat of Stacy's truck, I tried to contain the tidal wave of emotion that was trying to break through. She looked over at me and saw that I was trying not to break down in her space.

"Aaron, you need just to let all the emotion out. You have been so strong for so long, it's time for you to let it out. I won't tell a soul."

That was all I needed to just let the tears flow like a waterfall. The pain was such that I was shaking and sobbing. I lost control and just let the pain flow. It must have been hard for Stacy to see because she rubbed my back, my arm, and even my neck to try and calm me. We drove up to where we met up with Nick and I heard Jason over the radio, "Nick, it's Jason. We are at the spot. We appreciate you and the boys for doin' this. Over."

I sat up and wiped my face with the bottom of my shirt. Stacy regained her composure and if I didn't know any better, I do believe she was also crying. I'm sure I saw her wipe away some tears.

The radio crackled to life, "Howdy Jason and crew!

We will be at your location shortly. ETA is ten minutes. This is how things are gonna go. I will be in the front. Josiah will find a mid-point and slide in there and Jeb will take up the rear. We don't expect trouble from this other family, but you can't ever be too careful. Do you understand how this is going to go? Over."

"Yes sir. We won't even get out, we can make sure everyone is in line and just get rollin'. Again, thank you and your family for everything. Over."

"Not a problem, Jason. Thank you for being a stand-up group of youngin's that we CAN trust. Pullin' up now. Over."

We sat waiting to see the two monster Rams go by us on their huge lift kits. I think their wheels were as big as our truck was tall. We heard one of the boys mutter they were ready and in place over the radio and we all started driving down State Route 186. The posted speed limit was between twenty-five miles per hour and thirty-five miles per hour but we were going at least fifty-five miles per hour the whole way, in silence, as if people were going to hear our conversations from their homes.

We whipped past the mom-and-pop pharmacy, the family-owned pizzeria, and the dental office on the main strip. Most had their windows busted out, some had been on fire and were still smoking a little, and other buildings were just as stoic as if it were a normal Tuesday and the world never ended a couple of months ago. We flew by the gas station that had quite a few broken-down cars at the pumps and spilling out into the roadway. Stacy took to weaving around broken-down vehicles like a seasoned racecar driver. I noticed that the buildings were getting fewer and the houses were starting to spread out between fields that were farmed. I wondered where this family that caused Nick's family problems was living. Just as I asked that question to myself, Nick squawked over the radio.

"Well kids, this is where we will start falling back. You kids have a good trip and stay away from people. It was nice to meet ya. Please don't forget us. I don't mean anything by this, but I hope I never see you kids again. Over."

"We understand Nick. Thanks again. Over," Jason replied.

As we took off down State Route 186 towards State Route 15, I saw our escorts turn their vehicles around and all of a sudden, I saw the small puffs of smoke from gunfire. I heard it second. Stacy ducked inside the cab of the truck and looked over at me.

"Nick and the boys are under fire!" I yelled at her as she slammed on the brakes and jumped on the radio.

"Jason, Nick and the boys are under fire. Should we go help?"

"Don't you dare. This is what happens every day when we come this way. These damn rednecks in this house always do this. That's why we wanted to escort ya. Get goin', we can handle them." Nick blurted over the radio. I forgot Nick had a radio tuned into our channel.

"You heard him. Let's roll," Jason said.

Stacy and I started to catch up to the rest of the crew who was well on their way. I was secretly glad that Nick didn't need us to stay and help. I just had enough excitement for one day. I lost all my things to a mysterious fire that happened while I was sleeping. I leaned over on the passenger door window and let the truck lull me to sleep while Stacy drove us down the road to our next stop. Wherever that may be.

4.

I was jolted awake as Stacy slammed on the brakes.

"Did you see that? Of course not, you were sleeping, duh. I swear I saw a dog run across the street between Dan and Freya's RV and my truck."

I sat up so I could look out my side to see if I could get eyes on the dog. Then I realized as I woke up that I didn't know what kind of dog I was looking for. "What kind of dog, Stacy?"

"It looked like a German Shepherd to me. It was too fluffy to be a Malinois. Oh Lord in heaven if you're listening, PLEASE, let me get this dog."

Ever since we were at the house on Central Avenue in Toledo, Stacy has been secretly stressing about the dog that may or may not have been there. We all saw the bowls there in the house, we saw the dog food on the list and assumed that Brian kept the list just as he had kept his wife's clothes in the closet. We never found a dog, and Brian never told us about a dog, so we again assumed that there was no dog anymore. That the shopping list was old and the pet was gone just like the wife. Stacy just wanted the dog to be ok. She confided in me at one point that she was hoping that we would see some wildlife out there. It was eerily quiet and she said that the animals didn't deserve this. She asked me questions like did I think that the animals were immune like in the movies, or did I think that they are all hiding until things die down and the world gets to a new normal. I had no answers for her.

"Jason, we need to stop. Over," Stacy said as she was pulling over.

"Did ya blow a tire? Over."

"NO! I saw a dog. Over," she slammed the truck into park and jumped out without even checking her surroundings.

I jumped on the radio, "Uh, Jason. She took off to the left of our position. I was sleeping so I didn't see the animal. Over."

"Ok, Aaron. Do you have eyes on her? Over."

"Um, no. She ran into the tree line. Over."

"Take the radio, follow her. Everyone else, just stay in place. Over."

"Jana to Jason, I would like to help Aaron. Over."

"Fine. Meet him at his vehicle and go in together. I don't need three missing people. Over."

Jana met me at the truck and we were headed off across the barren street towards the tree line when Stacy came out with a big, beautiful German Shepherd in tow. We let out a collective sigh as we saw her.

"I told you! I knew I wasn't crazy!" Stacy yelled as she escorted the huge hound across the street to meet us. "She is super friendly and a bit skinny. She needs a bath but she otherwise is healthy. I am keeping her."

"Oh my god! This is splendid!" Jana said, kneeling to pet the newest member of our clan. "Oh look! She has a license!"

"Bet you'll never guess where she is from," Stacy said with excitement in her voice. Without giving us a chance to guess, she blurted out, "SHE'S BRIAN'S DOG!"

"Wait, how is that possible?" Jason asked as he walked up to the rest of the group. Dan and Freya were on the ground loving the dog with Jana.

"Well, remember Brian said he had to walk from the Bowling Green area? This, where we are, is in between Bowling Green and Findlay. If he brought the dog with him, it would make sense that the dog took off running because she was scared. She needs some food and some toys. She deserves a ball or two just for having to be out here to fend for herself. Oh, her name is Valkyrie! At least that's what the tag says." Stacy explained the appearance of the dog, pretty much that she was keeping her, and the way the dog was looking at her, this was a mutual infatuation. "Ok, I got her and we can go now. Aaron...," Stacy started to say as she was checking over the beautiful, but skinny, black and tan german shepherd.

I interrupted, "Yeah, I'll ride with Jason. If that's okay with you," I looked at him as I said it. Jason nodded his head in agreement. It's not like I had anything to transfer over. I swear I never saw Stacy as happy as she was right then as she ushered her new travel partner into the front seat of her truck.

I climbed in with Jason and Jana, Freya and Dan got into their vehicles, and back on the road we went. We stopped, turning left onto State Route 15 going towards Findlay, Ohio. When we got into Findlay, Stacy radioed that we needed to either stop at a pet store or at a Walmart to get her new bestie some necessities. We all decided that a pet store would be better because we would probably encounter fewer of the undead there.

Jason and I pulled off as soon as we saw a pet store that could also accommodate all our vehicles and would be easy to leave and get back underway. We were already wasting precious time by stopping. We saw a pet store in a shopping center off State Route 15, right where Interstate 75 intersected. We knew we would not be taking that way any time soon. Cars were hanging over the cement barriers and even though this apocalypse happened three months ago, there were still cars smoking. Either they were new wrecks or just that terrible that they were still smoking. Jason told everyone to stay back while he and I pulled up to the door to clear the way for Stacy to get what she wanted for her new friend.

Holy shit, the whole front of the store doors was splattered with dried blood. I looked over at Jason and he just sighed heavily while putting the truck into park. We exited the truck, melee weapons in hand. Jason was also strapped with heat, a 9mm Smith and Wesson on his hip. He was always carrying. Even in the house, when we had a house.

The automatic door slid open as we approached which scared the shit out of us. We had our bat and machete ready as we entered. We stopped at the entrance once we made it in so our eyes could adjust and the doors closed behind us. The lights inside were dim as if the generator for the location was not working at full power. When the doors closed, that's when it hit us, the stench of death and shit with a slight smell of swamp water.

I looked around, the cash registers to the right smeared with blood and other gore I wasn't sure I could identify, then aisles of dog and cat treats. In the midway displays, dead center was the displays with stupid little outfits and festive toys for the corresponding holiday which was St. Patrick's Day because that was the last holiday before the dead walked and spattered their vile all over the outfits. Next was the fish and aquariums which is where the swamp smell was coming from. The tank water was dangerously low and a color green I had never seen water be. One could see clumps of algae floating in the water that was left. Finally, looking to my far left were the rat and hamster cages and displays. The round showcases, that would have live animals that a child could see the animals run around in and pick out their favorite, were in front of the cage displays. There was nothing but blood and fur smeared on the glass. Whatever animals were in there, they were no more.

Jason scared me and made me jump when he spoke, "Well, I don't want Stacy to see this. Let's grab some food and stuff that wasn't bled on for Valkyrie and let's take it out." I nodded in agreement and grabbed a cart that was waiting to the right of me past the checkouts.

I ran over to the big bags of food with Jason following and watching my six. I went over to the dog food and grabbed a couple of huge bags of food, hoping it was good enough. I then went to the snacks and got the dog a large number of treats as I figured Stacy would want to spoil Valkyrie. It was easy to knock off the shelves of the bags with blood and gore on them. We turned around in the same aisle to grab some toys. It wasn't as easy as it sounds. We weren't sure how the animals reacted to the virus so we didn't want to give the dog any toys with possible traces of blood. While we were deciding which toys to get the dog, we heard a guttural moan and then shuffling of feet.

Jason put his index finger to his lips in a "shhh" motion and started walking down the aisle toward the back of the building. He got to the end and looked both ways. He saw nothing, I presume, because he then looked at me and mouthed to throw something. I grabbed a hard plastic toy and threw it over the aisle toward the back right corner of the store. I heard it hit the walker and then the floor. I started laughing, covering my mouth and nose with my hand. Jason almost passed out at the end of the aisle after looking at me like he couldn't believe I did that. The walker's location was identified so Jason regained his composure and went after the undead. All I could hear as I grabbed toys was the *THWAK* noise that a machete makes when connecting with flesh and bone. I decided that cart full of dog crap was plenty for the animal at the moment. I went to the front and waited for Jason.

Jason walked up to the front with his machete down to his side. He looked in the cart then looked at me and whispered, "Did you get bowls for food and water or were you expecting the dog to drink out of water bottles and use a fork?"

"Oh, FUCK!" I whispered loudly. Jason slapped me on the back of the head. Normally, I would have punched him right in his shit, but I couldn't. It was totally my bad.

"I got it," Jason said and walked down the midway to where the bowls were and grabbed a couple. He came back to the front with a leash as well.

We walked out the front door, took the cart to our vehicle, and loaded it all up. The radio was accidentally left in the cup holder and went off with everyone trying to check our status.

"Shit, sorry guys. I left the radio in the truck. We got everything the dog will need and are loading it up into our truck since we have room. Over," Jason answered the concerned group.

"Jesus, Jason! We weren't sure what was going on. I wanted to pick some stuff out for her. Over," Stacy said, a bit more excited than she meant.

"Uh, Stacy, it was best you didn't go in there. Over." Jason retorted.

"Oh. Well, thank you then. Over," sadness could be heard in Stacy's voice.

5.

"That damn Nick and his crew! They know they are supposed to call up to William when we find survivors." Sonya said to her husband. His name was Jerry but everyone called him Sarge in town before the apocalypse. Sonya and Sarge met William through The Federation.

William and his boys, Robert and Justyn , did a few things in preparation for this virus before releasing it in Toledo. They went to the towns around Toledo and when they couldn't get to the target areas or were running out of time, they conversed with people over the radio. Their directions were to catch any survivors, and if they couldn't, they were to notify them of any survivors passing through.

Jerry and Sonya met Robert when the boys split up to cover more ground. Robert helped them get a ham radio set up and explained to them what the survivors were going to be used for when he told the couple about the plan. Robert spent a week getting

Jerry and Sonya prepared for the virus. Robert also told them before he left that if any of The Federation found out that they were not holding survivors to be either converted as helpers of The Federation or turned into their zombie army, Robert would personally come down and gut them like the cattle they were. Ever since that talk, Sonya was more than the perfect little soldier.

Jerry didn't take too well to being told what to do. He let Sonya do her thing for what he called "The Cult" and he stayed out of it. Jerry wanted to stay alive, just sit on his property, and be left alone. He didn't want to be responsible for anything in particular. He just wanted his beers and his magazines.

Sonya was regularly out on supply runs at least once a week and she would bring back cases of beer and stacks of magazines for him to read, he didn't have a preference. The Maxim magazines he liked to look at the girls and make fun of all the meathead articles. "Want bigger biceps? Do this to maximize your protein usage" or "Low libido? Try these pills. Wife and girlfriend approved!"

He loved survivalist magazines to learn how to make generators from old parts lying around the house and how to cultivate his survival garden. None of the information was ever something he acted on. He did attempt to build a homemade hot water generator but he was drunk when he started it and got so frustrated with having to heat the copper pipes to form them into whatever the diagram showed that he dropped what he was doing and went to his favorite chair in the living room and just drank himself to the point of blackout drunk. He woke the next day telling Sonya that she needed to go on a run to get him more beer and he didn't care what kind it was as long as it wasn't them damn sissy white fist or talon or bear or claw. He wasn't a hipster and he refused to drink those "lame" fizzy drinks they tried to pass off as alcohol. That turned into an argument because, in Jerry's mind, 'The bitch needs to just listen and know her place.'

"I have to call Robert. I want him to know what the hell is going on," Sonya said to Jerry. She was in the living room, standing behind his chair while he read some magazine on football.

"Sonya, I have told you a million times, you do what you gotta do with them crazy people to keep us alive. I want no part in it. You got us into this, I expect you to deal with it." Jerry grabbed his can of piss water and took a hefty swig.

"Jerry, I need help with them survivors we got out back. They are requiring more and more food and I can't get it all. I cleared out all the stores near us and I'm gonna have to start goin' out farther to get supplies."

"I told you, woman," he began as he attempted to turn his rather large belly so he could face her and she could see the seriousness in his eyes, "I AIN'T DOIN' SHIT FOR THEM PEOPLE!"

"Fine, you fat fuck." She waited till he turned back around in his plush chair and not only shot him a nasty look but also pulled back her fist at him as if she were going to punch him in the back of the head. She thought better of following through as she realized it would hurt her more than him. Sonya went to the radio room.

The radio room was the only room in her house not occupied. Her two adult sons, Randall and Steve, shared a room and she had her room as Jerry slept in the plush recliner chair that he was always in. The boys did help her out on supply runs a lot, but they complained about it because they were starting to have to go out twice a week and it was getting more dangerous. Sonya closed the door to the radio room so she didn't disturb the boys' sleeping.

"Robert...come in...this is McComb watch...over." She waited a few minutes before repeating.

"Come in McComb watch...this is Home Base...over," a female voice that Sonya never heard before answered her call. Who cared who answered? She needed to report these people right away.

"Home Base... we have some survivors that got out of town going toward Findlay...over."

"McComb watch...how many and what were they using as transport...over."

"Home Base...they have trucks with trailers attached and RVs...over."

"McComb watch...how many...over."

"Home Base...I saw four vehicles...over."

"McComb watch," now a male was on, "do you know how many people were in there? Was one truck a big ol' Dodge Ram? Over."

"Home Base...that's an affirmative...over." Sonya felt so cool speaking to the main people in Ohio for The Federation. She wanted to move up in status and she figured this was the best way.

"DAMMIT!" the male voice from home base yelled over the open mic. "I am coming down there now. I should be there in a few hours if I can find a clear route...over."

Sonya started sweating. She wasn't sure if she was in trouble or not. Whoever was on the ham sure was angry and that made Sonya look bad, too. She knew it wasn't her fault, but she also knew that The Federation wasn't a bunch to mess around with. She better get the house in order for guests and tell Jerry to behave. The boys would have to go on a run alone to feed the people they did have in the barn. Can't have them dying before they're asked, more like required, to pledge their allegiance to The Federation.

6.

Jason and I climbed in the truck, sick to our stomachs because of what we had just seen. It's one thing when that happens to humans, but to animals, that hurts my heart. The animals didn't ask for any of this. They just tried to live and humans have screwed all that up for them. Valkyrie is the only animal we, as a group, have seen alive.

"Whoa, that was rough," Jason said. I'm not sure if he felt the need to state the obvious or if he didn't know what to say.

"Yeah, I'm glad we took care of it so Stacy didn't have to see that. So, after seeing the highway, what is the plan? Do you think I will be able to stop and grab some clothes and toiletries?" I asked meekly. I didn't want to cause any problems.

"Oh, shit, yeah! We need to do that. Probably for everyone. Great thinking!"

Jason got on the radio and told everyone we would need to do a human supply run. If they needed things, they better get them now while they could. Jana got on the radio and said there was a Walmart right behind the parked convoy. Everyone decided that would be the easiest way to resupply and agreed to just turn around.

Dan and Freya agreed to wait in the RV with it running by the door. The rest of us parked farther away. Jason and I were the first out. Stacy took Valkyrie to Dan and Freya's RV in case they had to leave fast. Everyone was on the side of the RV where they couldn't see the front of the store. Dan radioed that the front looked clear from what he could see. Dan and Freya were going to wait in the rear living part, not the cab part, in case some people had the same idea as they did and wanted to complete their supply run at the same place. Dan could see them coming AND warn everyone inside via radio.

Jason led the group with almost perfect precision up to the door of Walmart. The power was off in this store making it difficult to see inside. Jason was first, equipped with his 9mm and a machete, Stacy was next, also equipped with a machete and a shotgun, I was third with my baseball bat, Jana was watching our backs like an expert equipped with a shotgun in hand and a machete on her hip. Jason holstered his 9mm and pried open the front doors easily enough. They stayed open as we all filed in one by one. Jana closed them behind us, squeezing the doors together as I held her shotgun. She turned to me to grab her shotgun and stood at the ready. We waited at the front entrance listening to the sounds that were piercing the dark interior of Walmart. There were some distant bumping noises, items falling, and a couple of groans here and there, but it wasn't anything we couldn't handle.

We were quietly huddled as Jason gave us directions, whispering, "We can break up into two teams. Jana and Aaron, you start over in clothing and move over to personal care and pharmacy. Stacy and I will get food and swing around the back of the store over to camping equipment and ammo. Jana, put your radio close to your ear and turn down the volume. Aaron and Stacy, you two should turn yours off. Meet back here so we can go out as a team. If you run into trouble, silent kills only. Do not use firearms inside the store." We nodded in silent response and grabbed carts.

Jana and I started in men's apparel as I shut down my radio and Jana moved hers to her shoulder and turned the volume down. I needed new everything since my rig mysteriously went up in smoke. I went through and grabbed underwear, tee shirts, pants, shorts, and some socks. We then went over to the pharmacy area where we grabbed a lot of different toiletries like toothbrushes, toothpaste, deodorant, bath items, and hair care products. We then went behind the counter in the pharmacy. As we walked up to the door, we saw the door was already busted open. Jana and I just gave each other a look accompanied by an eye roll and had our melee weapons at the ready before opening the door.

Making an entry into the back half of the pharmacy was easy. We waited by the door to make sure we didn't hear any groans which would signify zombies in the area. All was silent. We walked further in and saw the mess left behind. The safe with the painkillers inside was open and cleaned out. We checked where the antibiotics were, all were still there.

At least we knew the drug market in the apocalypse was still in full swing. We grabbed the reusable shopping bags and filled them with all different types of medications from the shelves. If we didn't need them, they may be valuable for trade at some point.

"Hey, Jana. Check this out!" I motioned her over to an area where there were a few different books on the counter. They were books about medications and dosages. They also had information about drug interactions. "We should take these. None of us are doctors and we have no clue what we just grabbed off the shelves."

"You're right, kid. Smart thinkin'. Grab them and let's go. I just got a message to meet at the front," Jana said, smiling from ear to ear. I grabbed as many bags as I could in one trip and put them in the cart. I had to make two trips. We weren't coming back and knew there wasn't much hope for survivors as we hadn't seen any on the way. We may have been a bit greedy by taking all those meds but we also were thinking if our group got bigger, or one of us got sick, we had no way to heal ourselves quickly. Let's face it, plants work wonderfully but can only do so much.

Jana and I reached the entrance where we came in and saw Stacy and Jason waiting at the front for us with some interesting facial expressions. "Honeymoon's over or trouble in paradise, what's your guess?" Jana said to me with her eyes on them.

"Trouble for sure. Stacy looks like she hates every second she has to stand there with him, alone," I said to Jana quietly as we were approaching.

Jason turned to open the doors and Stacy had to stop him to remind him to call Dan to see if it was clear. He shook his head like he was in disbelief that he didn't think of that, radioed Dan, and was given the all-clear to proceed. We left out of Walmart and walked out to our rigs. Except me, of course. I now had to bunk with Jason. Dan and Freya pulled up to where we had parked away from the front door and let out Valkyrie, who ran over to Stacy as if they had always been together. We loaded up our rigs, and I made a home for myself in Jason's. While I was putting things away, Jason came up to me and said that at the next RV lot, we were gonna find a rig for me. He wanted to get out of the city first though. I nodded in agreement and had a smile on my face. He did care about my comfort.

These people were the closest thing I have ever had to family. They looked out for me, taught me things, and never made me feel like I was a burden. This must be what normal families are like. I had only ever known people who would make me feel like I was in the way or that I threw a wrench in their plans. I hated thinking about the past, but they made me think about it a lot and not because the new family was nasty. They were so good to me and it made me think about how bad it was when I was a kid. If I were treated like this while growing up, would I have ended up in jail so many times? I will never know but I think the answer is no.

We started our rigs, left the parking lot at Walmart, and headed back on State Route 15 toward the south. We had enough food and snacks to keep us fed for a while. Knocking off Walmart for their food, or what was left of it, was the best idea we had. The bread was now molded on the shelves, the milk went sour a long time ago, and the decomposing fruit brought almost as many flies as the stench the walking dead brought, but there were plenty of non-perishable foods on the shelves that were still good.

We left State Route 15 and went south on State Route 68 going toward Arlington, Ohio. While driving, we would see random zombies walking near accidents that we would have to maneuver around, going into the grass median at times, making travel very slow. We almost had Dan and Freya's rig get stuck a couple of times. Stacy had to gently push them from behind with her truck which gave her a flat tire and we had to roll at a snail's pace to Arlington which cost us valuable daylight. It wasn't her fault, and I'm not blaming her, but it was just one more setback we didn't need.

In Arlington, Ohio, after what seemed like an eternity, we found some mechanic shops on the main road. The first one did not have a tire her size. We walked to the other shops and by the third one, we found the tire we needed for her. Jason and I took turns rolling it back to where everyone else was waiting. We got back to see some zombies dispatched around the vehicles and Jason got worried.

"You guys ok? What the hell happened?"

"Relax, Jason," Stacy said. "They came out of the shop and we took them out quietly. One looked weird though which has us stumped. Come here and look." She walked over to the shop's overhead door to show him this huge male, eyes open and completely orange irises with flecks of brown and yellow, the whites of his eyes turning red from blood and the pupils dilated because he was dead. He had a deformed head and neck that looked like he was boiling from the inside and the steam bubbles couldn't escape the red skin. His veins were easy to see and were dark red. Under the skin, in the visible veins, things were crawling and traveling the venous system.

"Oh. My. God. STACY! It's just like the things we saw crawling under Brian's skin back at the house!" I exclaimed a bit too loudly.

"Holy shit, you're right! They have the crawly things, too!" Stacy said.

"What the FUCK are you guys talking about?" Jason asked.

I had to explain what Stacy and I saw back at the house. Stacy interjected when she had something to add and Jason was trying to remember if he had heard about it when they put Brian's corpse behind the barn.

"Why am I having a hard time remembering this?" Jason asked.

"I don't think I told anyone. We saw that the flies weren't attacking his body and that's when we noticed his skin crawling," Stacy said, trying to make Jason understand that he wasn't crazy or forgetful. "We also had no idea if it was even what we saw when we did." Stacy added.

"So," Jana stared at the dead monster on the ground, "the problem is a virus and it is mutating. Great. This means we will never find a cure if we ever get labs up and running again. Assuming this is nationwide."

Freya looked at Jana and asked, "Why do you think that?"

"When this is all said and done, hell, let's even say there still are labs open and functioning, do you think they will have the original specimen to work with? They need the first infected. They can make a cure or vaccine from that, then they can start making other variant vaccines as well. We have now witnessed eye color changes and body modifications, which to me means it is mutating fast and evolving into a superbug. However, I am not a doctor and never played one on TV."

Jana's response had everyone giggling first, thinking second, looking at each other third, then down at the new monster fourth. How are they going to combat something they can't see AND all its evolutionary family members? This is when we realized that not only were we all boned, but there may never be a way out of this mess.

7.

Robert jumped into the good truck as his dad was chasing after him from the house. William was told what Robert was doing after Robert walked out of the house in a hurry. Robert's sister, Brittany, had snitched on Robert that he was leaving without backup. He went down to McComb to take care of the people he didn't finish off in Bowling Green when he saw them. Now, Robert had a score to settle and in his mind, it wasn't gonna be pretty. Robert had been getting practice with other people that he had to dispose of within The Federation. People who he knew personally and they had not been doing the job required of them. They had not kept his promise to the family and The Federation.

William finally caught up with Robert as he was climbing into the truck. "Robert, where are you going?"

"Dad, there are these people that I thought I took care of in Bowling Green. I found out they are alive and the zombies didn't get them. I need to tie up loose ends before the next wave of the plan is implemented."

"You didn't stick around to make sure they were handled?"

"Dad, no. Not now. I am going to take care of it before they get too far. I either want them as my slaves or as my prize zombies. Tell Pamela to get moving on the next level of the virus and by then I hope to have our first subjects to test out our ZOM-GEN virus. You are always saying I need to man up, so let me get this done." Robert closed the door in William's face, started the truck, rolled down the window, and finished with, "The longer I stand here explaining to you, the longer they have to get a huge head start. Let me go take care of this." He didn't wait for his dad to acknowledge him, he didn't wait for an answer, he just rolled up his window and backed out far enough to be able to turn and drive out of the driveway onto the main road.

While driving out to McComb, Ohio, Robert was getting angrier by the minute. Thinking about all he had done to get where he was in The Federation and these idiots were going to ruin it. He just wanted to get these people to either agree to be part of the New Order or he would force them to become part of his zombie army. They would then unleash the horde into the populace and make them pick between salvation with The Federation or death by zombie, only to get up and walk the earth for all eternity. He knew he should have lit their rigs on fire before he left. The only reason he didn't like them was because they answered to no one. They were not controlled, and being uncontrolled made them a liability to the cause. Before he realized it, he had made it out to Sonya and Jerry's house. He pulled in and saw Sonya standing in the driveway with her shotgun pointed out at the truck.

Sonya saw Robert getting out of the truck and put the shotgun down to her side. "Hey there, Robert. Thanks for coming."

"Sonya, the fact that I am here is not good for you," Robert yelled back to Sonya, not giving a shit that she had a shotgun on her person. Robert was feeling pretty strong with adrenaline rushing through his veins. What made him feel even more powerful was when he saw her cower at his response. He was on top of the world right now and no one could stop him.

"I'm sorry. I thought you would want to know that they got away and that I called the second they made it out of town."

"Who helped them?" Robert asked.

"There is this family, the Foulks. They are refusing to help us help you. They don't want to see you succeed. They want to knock down The Federation. They don't want you to win." Sonya was angered by her neighbors not helping the cause. She was even angrier that they were able to live. The Federation was not usually this generous with people who refused to join the cause.

"What The Federation does is not up to any of us. Let's focus on the people that left the area. You said they were pulling trailers? Where were they going?"

"They went toward Findlay. They may be there by now."

"Ok, I am going to go that way. You stay here and watch that family. Let me know if they do anything. Do not contact my dad. I am handling the situation."

"I will, sir. Do you want to take the people I have locked up when you come back?"

"I'll worry about them if I have time." Robert got into his truck and left, following the directions that Sonya gave him.

Robert was tired after driving so long. He wasn't sure that he would catch up with them but he knew they would need to stop and he didn't. These people made a mockery of him and he didn't like being made to look like a fool. This was what angered him about society. This is why he felt so strongly about The Federation. They fell in line with his beliefs.

Coming up to the end of Findlay's city limits, Robert had wondered if they had made it through or if they had stopped somewhere. Robert decided that he would keep going. He had a bit of daylight left and even if they were staying in Findlay for the night, he would be able to set himself up somewhere in the next town so he could see them go by in the morning and follow them. Maybe he would act like a survivor and try to infiltrate their operation and see what they knew. Robert saw State Route 68 going south to Arlington and figured that would be a good place as the group he was hunting would need to go through that area if they wanted to get further south. Robert took State Route 68 south and hoped to set up camp in a shop that still had stuff available.

Not long after turning onto State Route 68, Robert encountered all the accidents and stopped cars on the road that the group had encountered. He was able to maneuver through them with ease because he just had the truck without anything being pulled behind it. It took him no time to come up to the small town of Arlington, and he was able to see the caravan of trailers, trucks, and RVs that the exact group he was looking for had. Robert pulled off to the side hoping that the group did not see him. He wanted to scope out the situation.

Who were these people? How many strong were they? Did they have weapons or any type of formal training? He did not see any army fatigues, which was a good thing. He watched them replace a tire on a big truck after rolling the thing halfway down the block.

He had to admit they worked well together as a group, but he needed them in his army. Whether the undead army or his human generals, he wanted them. They were strong. He could get them to rise against his father and then Robert could be the next in line for The Federation throne. As it stood right now, his father was next in line as The Federation president if something happened to that one and so far, it was not looking good for dear old Dad.

Currently, The Federation president was in a bunker with his most trusted followers. He had people like William out in the shit, but fortified so zombies wouldn't be able to get to them. Little did any of them know that Robert had his plans. No one had heard from the U.S. President in weeks. Last they heard, the President was staying in the White House because he didn't believe that he should be underground as his constituents were fighting the undead. Now the word was someone in his cabinet snuck out to see a spouse and got bit while trying to sneak back in and ended up infecting all of them. So, the United States may not have a president. He wasn't sure it was even a true story.

Robert was sitting there just watching how things worked with this group that he was following. He was learning their mannerisms and what frustration looked like in these people. He saw a tall skinny male and a shorter thin female with brown hair scavenging for useful things close by while a single dirty blonde male was doing the labor and replacing the tire. A tall, young, dark-haired, good-looking male was standing by the guy changing the tire and handing him tools. There was a tall blonde female who looked familiar to Robert and a dark-haired mixed female who was watching the back of the two working on the car. Robert thought women were only good for two things, feeding men and fucking men. He let a little laugh slip when he saw that the women were in charge of safety. After staring at the two women, he realized that he did know the tall blonde woman. He couldn't remember her name though.

The group finished up the tire replacement and cleaned up. They then got ready to make dinner for the group. To Robert, it looked like they were getting ready to settle in for the night. He also decided to eat some dinner. He was going to wait till they made a move and follow them. He wanted to own them and he would have to be smart, looking at the group and how they worked together, he was outnumbered and knew that it would need to be a surprise when he did make the move.

Robert waited and watched, watched and waited, and he was getting bored. He was hoping they would go to bed soon because he just wanted to sabotage their trip and go home. He was done with just sitting there. He felt like he could outsmart them so he decided to change the ambush idea and just get out and go up to talk to them. As far as he knew, they weren't a threat to anyone and he was certain that the woman he recognized wouldn't remember him. He wanted them on his team, though. They had survived under the radar for this long and he needed to know how. Robert got out of the truck quietly and out of sight of the group. He rolled around in the dirt to make it look like he had been on his own for a while and maybe they would welcome him in and he could find out what he wanted to know about the group.

After rolling around in the dusty drive of the abandoned building he pulled into, he checked his pockets for anything that wouldn't match his story and found the truck keys in his right pocket. He opened the driver's side door, tossed them on the floor of the truck, and quietly shut the door. He even used his knife to cut some holes in his jeans so he could make his story believable. He began his walk to the caravan, looking like just a guy with no supplies who was about to pass out. He was thinking to himself, 'A limp will sell it'.

8.

The group and I were inside Freya and Dan's RV, sharing a meal and making plans to head to Nashville. We had heard that there was a survivor compound there and wanted to see for ourselves, but also to get as far away from the hicks as possible. Valkyrie was sitting next to Stacy on the floor where she could pet the beloved pooch. Valkyrie had inhaled her dinner and was hoping that someone at the table would drop a scrap. All of a sudden, a low growl came from her and she stood at attention, slowly stalking towards the door. Stacy stopped the table from talking and we all watched the dog as she went to the door, ready to pounce. That's when Jason motioned for everyone to take a side and look out the windows. Stacy stayed by her dog, Dan and Freya took the north-facing side, Jason took the west-facing side so he could see the street, and I was up at the side facing the mechanic's shop. I was nervous because we had not seen anything since we dispatched the undead that were there when we arrived, so what could be making the dog on edge?

Jason had the answer. He saw a person walking down the road with a limp. He motioned to everyone that he had seen the reason the dog was going into protection mode. He walked to the table and quietly told everyone what he saw.

"I see a guy walking down the street, limping. I don't see any bites on him but he doesn't have a pack or anything with him, so I'm not sure what the deal is."

"We should just let him keep walking. I'm sorry but we don't do well with picking up survivors," Jana responded to Jason and then looked at the rest of the group.

I was standing closest to the window in the door and saw something out of the corner of my eye. "That's fine but what if he is trying to get into our trailers?"

"We will cross that bridge when we get there," Jason said.

I was still looking out the window watching this guy walk up to Stacy's trailer, reaching for the door. "Then we better figure it out because that bridge is here and Stacy is about to have a guy for a roommate." I couldn't watch much more because he was turning the door handle to her trailer. I swung the door open and jumped out with Valkyrie next to me, fur raised on her neck and back, growling, and her teeth were bared. I stopped short and had my bat out as the intruder began to slowly remove his hand from the doorknob. He was playing it smart by staying where he was, not turning around and not making any sudden moves.

"H-hey. I'm not here to harm anyone. I don't have anything. I-I'm just looking for a safe place," the unknown man said while still facing the trailer.

Jason followed behind me, then Jana. They flanked both sides of me. Stacy was directly behind me but could see what was happening. She then blurted out, "You're about to break into my home. I suggest you don't."

"Do you have any food or water you can spare?" the dirty man asked, still facing the trailer door.

"What's your name?" Jason asked.

"Don," the man lied. Robert was trying to sound as pitiful as possible, "PLEASE, I lost my family back in Findlay and have been walking for what seems like an eternity. I am hungry and thirsty. I will go after I get some."

Stacy whispered to me where Jason could hear, "I swear I know that voice." Valkyrie was not relaxing one bit.

Jason whispered to Stacy, "Recall your dog. Let's let him turn around."

"Valkyrie, here girl," Stacy said to the dog. The animal was torn between wanting to obey and wanting to protect. Valkyrie finally turned around and sat next to Stacy, not taking her eyes off Robert, the man who called himself Don. She could sense the lie.

"Turn around real slow," Jason ordered.

Robert turned slowly to his left to face the group. While turning, his right hand went down to his lower back where he hid his revolver. He was confident that the group hadn't seen it because they didn't walk up and take it from him. When he made the full turn, the gun was out of his waistband and partially hidden behind his leg. Robert was having a very hard time containing the smile that kept creeping across his face. Once he saw the group so far away and only with melee weapons, he felt very confident that he could take them all.

It was almost like slow motion, he turned, and Stacy's eyes widened. She must have recognized the man who called himself "Don". She yelled something I couldn't understand and I began to ask her what she was saying when the man lifted his right hand and got a shot off. The shot went wide to the right because he pulled the trigger too early. We all ducked, and then Jason pulled his 9mm out and took the shot at the right time, shooting Robert in the right shoulder. Robert jerked to the right, falling on his backside, and Valkyrie was on his throat. She grabbed onto the meat, shaking her head, tearing him to shreds. When Valkyrie decided she had neutralized the threat, she released him and went back to Stacy. Before we could even see what was happening, Robert was lying there dead, in a pool of blood.

We all looked at Valkyrie and it was almost as if the dog was proud of her work. Her muzzle was red with blood, she was panting, tongue hanging off to the side. Then we all looked at each other. "Good shooting," I said to Jason.

"Where are Dan and Freya?" Jana asked.

"I think they are inside the RV," Stacy said, eyes still as wide as when this all started. She knelt and started looking over Valkyrie who licked Stacy's face. "Eww, girl you need a bath and a toothbrush."

"What the FUCK just happened?" Jason asked while kneeling over Robert, trying to figure out what just had transpired.

"When fake Don turned around, I saw it was Robert, the guy from the truck back in Toledo. He started shooting and Valkyrie jumped into protection mode after you shot him, Jason." Stacy gave the play-by-play for those of us who couldn't keep up. That's when we heard the blood-chilling scream from the RV.

Stacy and Jana beat me and Jason to the RV. We saw Dan on the floor, blood pooled around him, his eyes open and a hole in his cheek. The wide bullet from Robert's gun had not been wide enough, and went through the RV window where Dan was standing and watching. All Freya could do was cry in her hands. Stacy and Jana encircled her, one on each side of her, and enveloped her in a big sister hug. We had lost a family member.

The girls moved Freya away from Dan, and Jason and I dug a hole with shovels we found in the shop. Freya couldn't stop crying. She had lost the love of her life. I couldn't help but shed some tears as Jason and I dug a hole to put our friend, no, our brother, in. We weren't supposed to be burying someone so young and full of life. He was killed because he was trying to keep his wife safe. He was not a fighter. He was a bookworm. A lover of plants, space, and humankind. He was supposed to outlive Jason and me. He was supposed to repopulate the world with all the good little hippy babies that he and Freya could make. I couldn't help but feel like we got him killed.

Jason and I finished the hole and we told the ladies. We all went to the grave site and said some nice things about the man we barely knew but considered a huge part of our little family. Jason and I lowered the body of Dan into the hole. Freya, being held around the shoulders by Jana, started to speak about her beloved.

"Dan taught me so much. When we met, we never

knew it was going to lead to this. After meeting, we were inseparable. We finished college together, then we got married and we found jobs together at the same company. We were never apart, and our love grew more and more for each other. We suffered through miscarriages and we rejoiced during promotions. We resigned ourselves to being just us as a family unit and we never left each other behind. Even in that death camp that was run by Robert's people, we stood at the fence, just looking at each other. When we escaped, we made vows to never trust people again until we came upon you guys. I finally saw life come back to Dan's eyes when he would chat with you guys about navigating from the stars or about structural integrity. He loved to teach because he loved people deep down. He loved with every fiber of his being. I am going to miss you, my beloved." Freya couldn't continue, the tears were flowing and her voice was cracking from sorrow and screaming.

We each had amazing things to say about the man who taught us so much with just his kind words and his patience as a teacher. He was one of a kind. As Jana was giving her tribute to Dan, we started filling the hole then the girls took Freya away from the scene, into Jana's trailer. Stacy began moving all of Freya's things into her trailer. Freya said she would not be able to drive that massive beast and she didn't want to stay in the place she and her love shared. We all understood and Stacy was quick to offer her place as a home to Freya. Jana and Stacy came out of the trailer after Stacy got the last load of Freya's things and Jason and I finished covering Dan's grave.

I walked over to Freya. "Here," I held out my hand to her and dropped the wedding band from Dan's finger into Freya's open hand. "I got this off him before we buried him."

"Oh, my goddess, that was so good of you. Thank you," Freya said, tears welling again.

"Now, what are we gonna do with that fat fuck?" I asked, nodding my head in the direction of the dead Robert. "We don't know if anyone knows where he is or if he even was alone. We don't even know how he found us." I was now concerned with the implications of killing Robert and if what Freya and Stacy said were true, we would have a whole encampment coming down on our heads.

"I don't even know. We should go ask Jason and see what he and Stacy have to say," Jana answered.

"Ask Jason what?" Jason said as he walked up to us.

"What should we do with Fat Fuck? We don't know if he's gonna change because we don't know for sure how the virus transmits. For all we know, it could be in all of us and airborne," I responded.

"Nah, it isn't airborne. If it was, there would be a lot more walking around," Jason said with confidence. "It has to be transmitted by bite."

"Ok, then think about this," Jana started, "Aaron brought up a banger of a point. Another thing we don't know is who knows he is gone. Will we have the whole hick community on our tails? Do any of his people even know he is down here? We need to pack up and go."

"That's what Stacy and I were talking about, as well. We should get going. I hate traveling at night, but we may have to tonight. We will need to take it slow because we won't be able to see. We can't drive with our lights on because it will be like a beacon." Jason was struggling with deciding and looking to Jana and me for help. We had no answers for him. He was the prepper of the group. We trusted him.

9.

William was getting anxious. He was pacing the house, waiting to hear from Robert. He thought in his mind about how Robert had stepped up and become a man he could be proud of and hand off The Federation legacy to. Tina was sitting in the living room watching William pace and finally said, "Sit down! You're making me anxious. Pacing isn't going to help."

"I can't help it. He should have been back or made a call by now," William responded with disdain in his voice. He hated it when Tina opened her mouth. He never knew why he married her in the first place.

"If you're that worried, get the McComb contact on the air and talk to that dumb bitch. What was her name?" Tina said, trying to pretend she gave a shit about the bimbo in McComb. She had suspected William had an affair with her a few months ago. She wouldn't put it past him. He was always trying to stick that small dick in a wet hole and he didn't care who it was.

"That's a good idea," William had enough of her

meddling. "Maybe I should find a woman who would help me with the operations of this plan. Oh, wait. I have a woman, she's just USELESS." He emphasized the last word while getting in her face.

Tina knew what he was doing and she didn't flinch. "Or, maybe, that woman should go off and find a different member of The Federation to be with. One with more stamina, that can last longer than ten seconds, with a few more inches of length," she said while continuing to read her book. She knew talking about his little manhood would piss him off and he would leave her alone. As prophesied, he stormed out of the living room to the radio room to contact Sonya.

"Home Base to McComb. Come in. Over," he waited impatiently.

"McComb here. Come in, Home Base. Over." Sonya's voice sang back. William and Sonya had spent many nights on the radio chatting about how much they cared for each other and how William was going to throw Tina to the undead if she threw Jerry to the undead so they could be together.

"What's the status on Robert? Over."

Sonya was a bit saddened by his straight-to-the-point tone. His wife must be there. "He was here and then went after the survivors. I haven't seen or heard from him since. Over."

William was perplexed. It was getting dark and William had taught Robert to never be out past dark. Robert would never miss a check-in. There were Federation members all over the nation and he knew where each safe house was in Ohio. "When did you see or speak to him last? Over."

"A few hours before dinner. Over."

William felt he needed to go find Robert but it was getting dark. He would send Justyn in the morning. "Ok. I will be sending a search party for him your way tomorrow. Be ready to house a few people. Homebase out." He got up from the seat and stared at the HAM radio for a moment. This was troublesome and had him questioning his son's intentions. He left to go find his other son and make him aware of the situation. He would pick good men, loyal to the cause, from the camp and they would go at dawn tomorrow to look for

Robert. Justyn agreed and went to round up his men from the work camp and get supplies ready for the expedition tomorrow.

"I'm taking Lee Edwards and Chris Sernik with me tomorrow. They are older, but I need wisdom and experience. I want to keep it as quiet as possible," Justyn reported back to William.

"Do you think they will be trustworthy?" William asked his son.

"Yeah. They haven't caused any issues in camp and they have proven to be hard workers."

"Well, they weren't exactly taken by their own free will. If you trust them, I will too. Good job son. Report back every two hours."

"No, I want to keep this as quiet as possible. They may have radios. I will report back to you once a day," Justyn insisted on secrecy and that was why William always had him out on raids. He was a tactical thinker.

"Ok, Justyn . However you want to do it. I just want to make sure I know where you are and that you're alive," William said as his heart sank thinking about the possibility that Robert was not alive. William left Justyn to get ready for the next day and turned in for the night.

Justyn , Lee, and Chris got ready for the trip just before the sun came up. They piled inside the other working truck on the compound and were off to Sonya's house in McComb. Lee and Chris were far from enthused. They didn't want to be at the compound, let alone going on recon missions with Boy Wonder looking for his brother. They were only on the compound working it because they didn't want to be part of the other group. They were also given the option to be loyal to the cause or get placed in a camp.

William's crew would do this three times. He would bring you into the house, give you the option, and if you said no, you were taken to the nasty camp. Captives were only fed once a day; the shitters were overflowing and illnesses were running through the camp. When the loyalists heard someone was sick from the camp, they would come and take the person away. No one knew where they went and no one ever saw them again. Only two people were known to have escaped and they were a skinny couple no one would have guessed would have been able to leave, let alone make it out there with the undead.

The recon crew finally got to Sonya's in McComb, Ohio. Lee and Chris had to get out and move a few cars out of the way so they could take the most direct route. They were tired and just wanted to rest. As they were moving the vehicles out of the way, it gave them time to chit-chat about what was going on with the camp, what they were doing with this fuck-boi, and why were they going to McComb.

"What's your name again? I'm normally not this bad with names but, I also normally eat more than what we have been given at the camp," Chris said with a chuckle.

Lee, chuckling also, replied, "I'm Lee. Neither one of us should be here. We were picked because we are expendable."

"No, jackass," Justyn yelled from the driver's window, "You were picked because you are both old enough to know better. Now shut the fuck up and get the cars moved."

Lee and Chris looked at each other and rolled their eyes. Chris said quietly, while gritting his teeth and acting like the car was tough to move, "I'm gonna kill that son of a bitch." Lee chuckled again under his breath and they kept on pushing. Knowing now that Justyn was listening, they kept their conversation at a low volume and without lip movements.

After a few hours of moving cars out of the way, the boys finally reached Sonya's house in McComb. Justyn , Lee, and Chris walked up to Sonya's house. She must have been looking out the window because she was out on her porch to meet them. Justyn just rolled his eyes. He hated this woman.

"Well, hi there, boys!" Sonya said, dripping with an ass-kissing tone. She looked like she hadn't showered in years. Her shoulder-length, brown hair stood up almost on end and in knots, her shirt looked like she dropped every lunch she ever had on it, and her blue jeans were so soiled they were brown and bore no resemblance to any of the previous color or fabric. Justyn could smell her even before she got close and wished the wind would blow in the other direction so he could be upwind.

"No time for your fake pleasantries. My dad isn't here so you can stop with the theatrics. I'm just here to find out where my brother is." Justyn said, cutting right to the chase. It made Sonya give him a look of surprise.

"I'm not sure what you mean about your dad, but I can assure you...," Sonya faked shock and surprise, lifting her hand to her chest as if she was just insulted. Justyn cut her off.

"Yeah whatever, bitch. Where the fuck is my brother? If I don't find him alive, my dad will only come here to throw you and your sorry, sack-of-shit husband to the zombies to be used as our zombie army. No longer serving us as a human. Do you understand, hoe?" Justyn was nose-to-nose with Sonya. She swallowed hard and began to explain, her voice cracking, showing her fear, how she only saw him for a minute and he then took off towards Findlay. She finished with, "I haven't heard from him since".

Lee and Chris were standing back, further away from the other two, and they could still smell Sonya. They were trying to cover their noses without being obvious.

"So, I was thinking while we were moving cars. What if we could get rid of Justyn ?" Lee started the conversation quietly.

"I was thinking the same thing, but I didn't want to put you in a predicament. What do you suggest?" Chris said, eyes straight ahead watching the interaction between Justyn and Sonya.

"I'm not sure how, yet. When I know, you'll know." Lee said just in time. Justyn was done talking to Sonya and was walking their way.

"Get in the truck, you fucks," Justyn said with an attitude that said he was two seconds from blowing up that chick's house if they didn't leave now.

Lee and Chris looked at each other, rolled their eyes, and climbed into the truck. Justyn slammed the driver's side door when he got in and looked at the two men. "We will come back here and blow this house up if I find my brother dead," Justyn said to them. They could see the white-hot rage in his eyes and feel the anger radiating off the man. The two unwilling travel mates nodded in understanding which was Justyn 's cue to leave.

Following what he thought were his brother's steps, Justyn and the two plotting riders rode south on State Route 68. Justyn had been speeding down the road, trying to beat nightfall. He had wasted so much time with that woman back at the house, he knew he would never get that time back. Coming up on the small town of Arlington, Justyn began to slow while he leaned forward in the driver's seat, squinting. Lee, who was sitting shotgun, tried to trace where Justyn was looking and when he saw it, his eyes widened. Justyn began pulling off to the spot where Robert parked the truck earlier.

Justyn looked over at Lee with a confused look and Lee silently agreed with him. Chris was popping his head up to the front from the back seat and saw what the other two were looking at. Chris glanced over at Lee who was doing such a good job playing the part that he deserved an Oscar. Justyn came to a stop and ordered the other two to grab quiet weapons. They did as instructed and waited for the word.

Justyn looked around, the other two followed his

lead. It was all clear so Justyn opened his door and the other two followed him. They slowly approached the truck, heads on swivels, but keeping below window height, just in case. Justyn reached the driver's door and looked back at Chris who had his bat at the ready, following him, and was now playing his role for his Oscar-worthy mention.

10.

We left Arlington after that Robert guy was shot and we lost our friend, Dan. We figured we attracted every walker in the area so we up and left. We buried Dan but left Robert out for the walkers to feast on as a diversion. Say what you will, it was a good plan. We left Arlington behind and were currently scavenging in an even smaller place called Williamstown.

Looking at Jana, I said quietly, "I'm not so sure we will find anything in this place. It looks smaller than Arlington!" Jana and I had been paired together to walk down the right side of the main street in this tiny town. Most of the buildings were all busted into, windows broken, doors left open, and to top it all off, it was getting late. Darkness was creeping up on us and we didn't get too far from Arlington. Six minutes away was not far enough for my liking.

"Yeah, I think it's a bust. We should go in here though." Jana stopped in front of a general store. The sign was split, General Store and Pharmacy. I stopped a few steps away, looking at the front of the broken-out building. The front door was open, glass was all over the sidewalk, and from what I could see, the shelves looked bare.

"OK. Throw a brick in there to see if anything makes a noise first. I don't want to be surprised," I said wearily.

Jana picked up a brick from the ground and tossed it into the store. We waited to hear groans, shuffling, or any noise indicating someone, or something was inside. We were met with silence. Jana had her trusty bat, Betty, with her at the ready as she went in and I had a crowbar I had picked up and decided not to name in public. My crowbar's name was Carl. He was a good friend.

I followed Jana into the general store. All the shelves at the front were empty. There were some items left on the shelves toward the back of the store. What I have noticed is that people didn't think vitamins and supplements, adult diapers, feminine products, and pantyhose were going to be necessary in the end times so they left them behind. Each place we went to, we saw those items still on the shelf. This store was no different. I began grabbing vitamins and supplements. I had read somewhere that certain supplements would help with all types of health issues. I didn't study the book so I wasn't sure which did what, so I just dumped all I could fit in a bag.

Jana found some cute toys for Valkyrie that she didn't have yet and put them in a bag for her. That dog was living the life. We were all enamored with her, if I was being honest. Jana also found some medicines that we would find useful. I'm not sure for what, but Jana said they were going to be useful and I believed her. We also found some single bottles of water and juice. Jana and I drank a couple of those for ourselves but we did take some to the rest of the group. We met back at the convoy and saw that this stop was useless. We felt a bit defeated but we had some good stores in our supplies. This was just a top-off mission and wasted valuable time.

"Ok, I have decided I am not making another decision to stop again," Stacy said with a chuckle. "Apparently, I suck at it."

We jumped into our respective vehicles and began driving south on State Route 118, turning right onto State Route 29. We crossed the state line into Indiana and let out a collective sigh. We found ourselves, a couple of hours later, ok, it was more like quite a few hours later, in Marion, Indiana, a small town that looked promising. We didn't see as many undead hanging around as we pulled into a truck stop to sleep.

In Jason's camper, I pulled out the sofa sleeper and Jason went back to his room. As I was pulling out the sofa, Jason said, "I haven't forgotten that we need to get you a place. We have just been a bit busy and haven't come across an RV place yet. If I was thinking, back when we left the RV, we could have had you take that."

"No, I would not have been able to sleep there knowing that it was Dan's. It would have been too weird for me. Ya know?" I replied to Jason as I finished making the bed. "I would rather just get a new one. Especially since all we have to do is take it."

Jason nodded in understanding and went off to bed. I laid down on the pull-out and just stared at the ceiling. It was hard to get to sleep after we had just lost one of our own and his spouse was still living. I finally was able to fall asleep thinking of all the cool things Dan taught us. We wouldn't have gotten this far without him and Freya. They were both master herbalists, they had a way with plants and anything they put their minds to. It was almost as if they understood right down to the very smallest atom.

The morning sun hit me right in the face. I heard everyone outside and thought Jason and I slept in. I got up, took a piss, and checked on him in his room only to find it empty. That SOB never woke me up. I got myself ready for the day and our travels ahead. I knew we would have a long ride to Nashville. I just hoped that the whole Nashville thing was real. It's a long way to travel on a little bit of overheard radio traffic conversation and hope. We hadn't heard anything about this place since moving on from Toledo. We didn't have our HAM radio anymore but hopefully, the closer we got, I hoped we heard SOME form of traffic.

I walked out to see everyone huddled around in a

circle, excited. I was standing at the door outside of the travel trailer, not awake enough to even comprehend what was going on, but I do know that I heard the radio squawk and Stacy talking back to whoever was on the other end. I walked past them over to the coffee. Thankfully, someone made a little coffee stand so we all could have our kickstart this morning. Apparently, I was the last one at the party.

"What did I miss?" I asked as I stood over at the coffee bar and began to wake up thanks to the brown liquid gold in my cup.

Freya came over to me, "We made contact with another group who said they were also going to Nashville. It's real! We are going to a survivor camp!" She was so overjoyed, the excitement was radiating from her in waves which made me get excited.

"I was just thinking about that last night. Like, do we even know that people are there, and just doubting the whole thing! I'm so glad! What are they saying?"

"They are coming from the other side of Indiana and had heard about Nashville. They are just as excited to hear from us. So, we are gonna try to meet up with them and Jason is working on the details of where. The only problem is, we will be waiting most of the time." Freya's enthusiasm waned but was not completely gone.

"Jason will make it work where we aren't waiting that long. He will keep the both of us moving and meet somewhere in the middle. I just hope they are like the others that we met back in McComb," I reassured Freya and myself. Jason had it handled.

Freya went back to the group that was around the radio and I saw that Stacy had handed the radio off to Jason. She must have decided that Valkyrie was more interesting. Jason had the map pulled out and was trying to find a good meeting point. I know absolutely nothing about maps or directions unless the cops are involved so I kept to myself and drank my go-go juice.

"THAT'S IT!" Jason yelled. He got all of our attention as he went back to the radio. "We are good to meet in Greensburg, Indiana!"

"Well, is that on the way?" Stacy asked as she stopped playing tug-o-war with Valkyrie. Valkyrie just stood there with the toy in her mouth, expectantly watching her new alpha.

"It is. We can wait in Greensburg for them. We will find a house or four on a block. We can set up a house or store a block or two away as a meeting point to make sure they are on the up and up. We should have time to clear a couple of houses for them to stay in if we find that we do like them and travel together to Nashville." Jason was excited to have a purpose.

"I like it. Let's get going. It won't be daylight forever." Jana said as she and Freya began packing up the coffee bar.

"Aaron," Jason started, "we will be looking for accommodations for you along the way. There are more camper dealers out this way so we should be able to find you something."

"Thanks, man. I don't mind, but I would be excited to be able to walk around naked." I chuckled and Jason made a face like he wanted to hurl.

All packed up and radio checks complete, we left, going down State Route 18, deeper into Marion, Indiana. As Jason and I were driving, he asked me to flip through channels to see if anyone else may be alive out there. I did as asked to only get back silence.

Traveling eastbound on State Route 18, we started to see a haze in the air. Jason and I looked at each other, confounded by the strange haze. It was morning and not very hot; pleasantly warm without a lot of humidity. It was after coming up out of the dip that we saw the huge pile of vehicles. Jason slowed and I got on the radio to let everyone know to stop.

We all got out, walked closer, and checked the scene. State Route 18 at Interstate 69 was a smoky mess. Cars, trucks, vans, and buses were a twisted burned mess. There was a semi that was hanging off the interstate onto the street below that crushed another car. It was hit by another semi, and possibly a car was in between them, but it was hard to tell. Smoke was still coming from different areas of the huge crash. The driver of the semi that was still on the expressway was a blackened being half hanging out the window. People had changed while driving away from the original cause, zombies in the road trying to chase down the vehicles. Some were still locked inside cars with windows down as the people were bit while waiting for the rest to move. Those couldn't get out because they were buckled in. Safety first, I guess.

We were walking through the disaster, trying to ascertain the situation and if we could move any of the blocking vehicles. Jason and a few of the others would put the strapped-in undead out of their misery by clubbing them or stabbing them in the head with their quiet melee weapons. I was trying not to throw up at the smell of burned bodies, decaying bodies, and some fuel mixed in with piss, shit, and burned rubber.

I walked up to a car and had a scare. All of a sudden, an arm shot out of the window of a car and tried to grab me. I turned to see an elderly man, now an undead, clawing for me through his open window. His bite wound was on his forearm, blackened, and no longer oozing anything. I could see the bones in his arm. It looked as if he had been bitten two or three times in the same area. His mouth was chomping at the air. He was buckled in and couldn't figure out how to free himself in his undead state. He was emaciated because he hadn't been able to feed. His skin, what was left that is, was blackish green and looked as if, had I touched him, it would just fall off his bones. The wind blew at that moment and the smell of excrement, urine, and decomposition wafted at me. I hooked his head with my sharp crowbar end because he wasn't hanging out of the car far enough for me to be able to swing the blunt side at him. Now, the crowbar was stuck and made a sickening sloppy suction noise as I wiggled it back and forth to try to remove it from his temple on the opposite side from where I was standing. Finally freeing it from the elderly man, I had to wipe off the end as best as I could on the only spot that was clean on the man's clothes. It wasn't exactly the best cleaning job I had done, but it would have to be good enough.

Before I kept moving toward the semi that had fallen over the side of the expressway, I looked around to get an eye on everyone. They were all doing the same thing as I was, putting the undead out of their misery. I walked up to the semi and Jason came up right after. We both just stared. The semi had pile-driven a car into the pavement and we could see detached arms hanging out of some windows of the pancake flat car.

They didn't suffer. They were, however, nibbled on by the undead. YUCK!

"I don't think we are getting past this," Jason said to me as the girls started to walk up.

"Nope. I am not moving all this. Can we go around?" Jana said, breathing heavily.

"I'm sure we can." Jason answered. He then turned around to go back to the truck and pull out the map. The rest of us followed to see the route we would be taking.

Jason pulled out the map and started looking. "Here it is, we can go back to State Route 3 and turn right to Muncie. It isn't a huge diversion. Just a few minutes."

I noticed the flames between Stacy and Jason weren't entirely cooled as she was standing so close to him from behind, looking over his shoulder that she could have put her chin on his shoulder. I wondered if he could feel her breathing on his neck. 'Stop you pervert!' I scolded myself in my head. She had made it very clear that this was the end of the world and no one should be worrying about their sex life more than making it through the day.

"Ok, let's get going so we can find a place to bunk down and resupply in Muncie. Do we know if this will take us longer to get to Greensburg?" Stacy said, backing up a little as she waited for Jason to turn around and look at her. He never did, he just answered her, still looking at the map. I guess things are ice-cold on his end.

"Nope. The time won't make a huge difference and if we don't hit another snag, we can make it up with speed on the road. They are so far that we would be bunking in town a few days before they got there, anyway," Jason absently told her as he focused on folding the map.

Everyone else, including myself, went to our respective vehicles to make the turnaround. We got everyone turned around and made the turn to go south on State Route 3. It only took a few minutes and we were in Muncie, Indiana. We pulled up to a Walmart, why is it ALWAYS Walmart?, and began checking the place out. It was full of walkers. We decided to find another store on State Route 3. We came upon a place called Royerson Food Mart.

Royerson's had a couple of cars in the parking lot that we noticed as we pulled in and that meant there were not a lot of people inside. We hoped at least. Stopping the vehicles along the back part of the parking lot, we all got out. Even Freya joined us with a bat that Stacy gave her. 'Wait, is that her beloved Betty?'

We walked up to the doors, two lines of us on either side. Jason and Jana crouched on the left, and me, Stacy, and Freya crouched on the right. Jason tapped the end of the ax he had acquired on the glass doors. Nothing moved. We stood up straight after we didn't get a response from the noise. Jason then began to pry at the doors, trying to open them. They wouldn't budge.

"I think it's locked. Maybe that's why no one is in there. Were they closed when the world went to shit?" Jason asked, looking at us as if any one of us were here that day.

"We wouldn't know," Stacy said in the smart tone she gave everyone. Was she salty about how Jason responded to her earlier like she was just one of us and not someone he cared deeply for?

"I'll go around back." Jason volunteered. AGAIN.

"And do what?" Stacy queried as her hands went on her hips as if she was his mom.

"Check and see if there is a way to get in. What else would I be doing?" Jason responded with a bit more aggression than I think he meant to.

"Not alone, you're not!"

Jason's face went red, "Ok, MOM! Who wants to go with me?"

Jana volunteered just to stop the brewing fight between the two. Jason looked at Stacy with an "Are you happy" look that made her fume. Jason and Jana turned to leave and, hopefully, go in through the back and let the rest of us in. Stacy watched them as they went around the corner then scoffed.

"I don't know why he thinks he needs to save the world," Stacy said, mumbling to herself more than looking for an audience. She was leaning on a railing that was by the front doors to corral people to the left so they wouldn't walk into a wall because they weren't looking when they were exiting the store.

After what seemed like an eternity, the front doors finally clicked. Jason was there unlocking the doors and getting ready to pull them apart because the power was off. Stacy stood up and looked relieved to see them. We disappeared into the store that looked untouched.

11.

Justyn pulled open the driver's side door real quick and got out of the way as Chris, bat held high over his head, looked into an empty truck cab. Keys were on the floor by the brake pedal. Chris slowly brought down the bat and bent over to grab the keys.

"No one's in there, but these were on the floor," Chris said as he handed the keys to Justyn .

"These are the keys to the truck. What was my brother doing?" Justyn wondered more to himself than to present company.

Chris looked past Justyn and saw a body. Pointing, Chris said, "Hey, over there, man. What is that?"

Justyn and Lee looked in the direction Chris was pointing. There was a body lying there, and a walker was munching on it. Justyn lifted the machete that he had and walked over to the walker, doing him the favor of removing his head from his body. The body fell, the head rolled over to the left, mouth still munching on the body. Justyn saw that the walker was making a meal out of his brother. Lee and Chris came over, saw it was Robert on the ground and began to get nervous because they assumed that he would get up and walk again as a walker.

"He's dead from a gunshot, you idiots. He won't get back up," Justyn said, kneeling at his brother's side, tired of the two that he had to bring with him.

The guys could feel his anger brewing. Chris took the moment; he raised his bat above his head as he was standing behind the crouching Justyn and brought it down on his head. Justyn was down for the count and Chris saw blood coming from the wound he had caused.

"Let's get out of here. Let the walkers get him," Chris said to Lee. Lee nodded in shock as Chris bent over and grabbed the truck keys from Justyn 's limp hands. The two went to the truck that Robert drove, since it was the better truck of the two, and took off going south on State Route 68. They didn't have a plan, but they knew there was nothing for them up north, so the two continued south.

A few hours later Justyn woke up with the worst

headache he could have imagined. He was lying on the ground next to his dead brother. Slowly, Justyn sat up. His head was spinning and hurt so bad that even holding either side of it with his hands, squeezing a little, wasn't making it any better. He looked to see his truck still there, but the truck Robert took, that was gone. He had been double-crossed and nothing made him angrier.

He thought to himself how lucky he was that he was out cold and didn't get bit. He felt his left pocket and found he still had his truck keys in his pocket. Lady Luck was on his side. He didn't want to push it so he decided to go back to Sonya's house and radio what he was dealing with at the moment. He needed to know who shot his brother and where they went. Then he would go off and find the two idiots that stole his brother's truck and hit him over the head. They were gonna pay with their lives but still be of service to the family and The Federation.

Justyn pulled into the driveway at Sonya's house, and as expected, she came out to meet him.

"I need to use your radio," he said to Sonya.

She walked him inside without any small talk, took him to the radio room, and left him so he could have some privacy. Maybe she learned her place, finally.

"McComb to Home Base, come in. Over."

" Justyn ? It's Dad. Over."

"Hi, Dad. I found Robert. It's not pretty. Over."

"Is he dead? Over."

"Yeah. The two idiots you sent with me hit me over the head and took the truck Robert was driving. Over."

There was an abnormally long pause. "Ok. John is on a run so I can't send him. Over"

"I don't need him. Sonya said she saw some people leaving town going that way so I am going to talk to that old man, Nick, that refused to help us. If you don't hear from Sonya that she saw me pass by in a few hours, we have a bigger problem than we anticipated. Over."

" Justyn , son, just kill that family. Blow their place up. Sonya has some munitions. This stops today. You hear me? Over."

"Yes, sir. Over."

Justyn wasn't afraid to do what was necessary for The Federation. He was already planning on blowing that family off the map. His brother was dead because of them. That was the assumption he was making. If that family hadn't let them people go, his brother would still be alive.

He left the room and walked out to Sonya, who was sitting in her kitchen at the table, completing a puzzle. Her husband was not in his usual spot, the chair.

"Where's your husband?"

"Oh, he went with me on a run and zigged when he should have zagged," Sonya said without even lifting her head.

"You don't seem too upset about it."

"I'm not."

"Well, I am going to take care of those folks up the street. My Dad ordered them exterminated. I need the munitions you have here."

"I will get you the box of grenades we have. The Federation gave them to us to hold for occasions such as these," Sonya said as she got up from her table and went to the basement. In just a few moments, she came back up with a box. Justyn was surprised she could carry it. It wasn't like they were being given a lot of food to maintain themselves.

"I'll take them from you. It looks heavy. I will drive by and honk the horn when I have set them and left. I will need you to get on the radio and tell my Dad you heard from me. If you don't, he will send people down here to lay waste to the whole town and that will include you. Please don't forget," Justyn said.

"I sure will."

"Oh, I'm sure you will," Justyn said under his breath as he turned and walked out the door to his truck. When he got the crate placed on the passenger side floor, he opened the top. No wonder the crate didn't feel too heavy, it was damn near empty! Justyn wondered what she was doing with the grenades. He knew The Federation gave them a full box. He kept the lid off, shrugged because what could he do about it, and went to the driver's side and got in. Off to Nick's house up the street to take care of that problem. Then he could go avenge his brother.

12.

William got so mad he threw the mic from the HAM radio. His son was dead and he knew what kind of shit parent he had been to him. He realized that he couldn't do anything about it now but his remaining son, Justyn , would take care of it. He would blow up all of McComb if he needed to. This was not going to mess up the plan that Robert had come up with. William refused to allow it to mess up the empire he had built with them.

William went in to give Tina the bad news. Their son was confirmed dead and Justyn , their other son, was looking to exact revenge on the people who did this. He should have told Justyn to wait so he could send out some people to help him, but Justyn was stubborn and would have refused to wait. That boy was exactly like his old man. He hoped that Justyn would at least call on the radio when he got to a safe house that was close to where the people he was hunting may be located.

"Tina, we need to talk," William said as he entered

the living room where she was, again, reclining on the couch reading another romance or erotica novel. She had made sure that she would never be without books as she cleared out the two sections in the nearest bookstore.

"What is it? I'm in a really good part of my book right now and you are interrupting."

William curled his lip at her. If he hit her, who would stop him? No one. He was the law; he was Judge Dredd. " Justyn found Robert."

"Well, good for Justyn . How is Robert these days? Still a daddy's boy?" Tina mocked the new relationship that William had with his boys. He knew he deserved this. He remembered beating Robert on multiple occasions and in all honesty, he didn't regret it. It made Robert the man he is today...or was. Robert used to cling to his mother for many years. It made William so angry with him that he would beat him just for doing that and being a sissy.

"I wouldn't know because Robert was found murdered. Justyn didn't give me many details, but he is currently in McComb setting up some munitions at that house that we went to a while ago to get them to send us survivors. Remember? They refused to help. A guy named Nick and his wife Jenn. Justyn is going to blow their house up and I am thinking I want to send people down there to help Justyn 'persuade' the two to give up information about the people they helped leave McComb."

"I told you that you should have killed them when they refused to help you." Tina had not looked up from her book once. "What are you telling me for? That was your baby. All I did was protect him when you tried to strong-arm a toddler, the big, strong man that you are. " She was again mocking him and how he raised the boys. If he didn't raise them the way he did, they would be pussies and not able to complete this mission. William saw the red deepening to almost black every time Tina brought up the past.

"Bitch, I will smack the shit out of you if you don't shut your mouth."

"Oh, there's something new," her face still in the book.

William turned and stormed out of the living room. He went out to the pole barn to see if John had come back from the run he sent him on. John was in the truck he was given by William. He had gotten a lot on the run and was found sitting in the front, sort of in the middle, but his pants were unzipped and he was getting a blow job from a female survivor he had found. William, watching and thinking he needed to take a ride out to McComb, waited till they were done before he made his presence known. When he saw the girl pulling her shirt over her head and John leaning back to button and zip his pants, William cleared his throat. John turned around to see William and the woman let out a tiny shriek because she was startled.

"Hey, William. What can I do for you?" John asked his father figure.

"I think I would like you and a couple guys that we can trust to go out with me to McComb. You up for it?"

"Always. What are we doing?"

"Well, son, we are gonna help Justyn get back at some people who killed Robert."

John's eyes went wide. "Robert's dead?"

"Yeah. Justyn found him and will be looking to get information from some people who know the people who may have done it. We need to go, like now."

John turned to look at the girl who just serviced him, "Get out, bitch. You heard him, we have to go."

When the girl got out of John's truck, William noticed she was a fine piece and he wouldn't mind taking a slice. William looked at the young woman and told her, "Go inside the house and tell Tina, she's sitting on the couch, tell her you're John's girl and she will get you cleaned up and fed. She will also show you to his room where you can wait in safety till we get back."

The girl was very underweight but William knew Tina could fix that. She was grateful for the care and concern. "John told me that you guys were nice. Thank you! Thank you so much!" Little did she know she was walking into a house that would be worse than H. H. Holmes' house of horrors.

John's face lit up as he understood what this meant. He could do what he wanted with her when he came back. His father figure, William, would also be able to have her when he wanted as payment, but she was John's to do with as he pleased. No longer a person or individual, now she was considered property and could be bartered if need be. People and possessions were the currency of this new world. Especially the new world The Federation created.

The girl went inside and William went with John to the barracks where the most loyal people were housed that were there from the start. John and William picked two people to go with them and had them get four bags ready of munitions. Once they were done, they all got into the truck with John driving. William had stopped driving as he felt that he was too good to drive in the apocalypse. William said it was a status thing.

William, John, and the other two males, Dwayne and Devon, were on their way to McComb. John thought now would be a good time to ask what the plan was.

"So, William, what's the plan? Do we know who these people are?"

"I know nothing. Justyn is asking a family that helped this group leave the McComb area. They got past our McComb contact, Sonya."

"OK, so are we meeting Justyn at the people's house? I think I know what family you're talking about and I know where they live. I was with Robert when they went to try to convince them to be part of The Federation. Isn't it Nate and Jean, no. Nick...Nick was the guy. Nick and Jess? No. Nick and Jenn maybe?" John was straining his brain for the memory.

"Yeah, I think it was the last one. Nick and Jenn. They are about to be questioned by Justyn , and I'm not sure but I think Justyn will blow the whole house up if they don't have the right answers. I'm not sure how much time we have so we better step on it," William said to John, insinuating that he was going way too slow for this.

"OK, Boss. I get you." John said, letting William know he understood what the father figure was telling him. John increased the speed and they made it to the McComb town limits in record time.

John pulled up in front of the home of Nick and

Jenn, seeing Justyn 's truck in the driveway helped. Everyone got out of the truck. William started giving directions to Dwayne and Devon.

"Double D, I want both of you to check the perimeter for munitions. I want to see if Justyn has had time to set them up. John, you and I are going to go inside and see what is going on. We need to find out if Justyn was able to get any information from these idiots." William always gave nicknames to people he knew he wasn't going to keep around or were expendable. Hence the two, Dwayne and Devon, being nicknamed Double D.

Double D went to Justyn 's truck and saw that the box of grenades was not empty. Devon asked William, "Do you know how many were in here? I only see six grenades in the box."

"I'll go ask that woman up the street. I need to talk with her anyway. Put those six out, there are more in our truck. Just set them up. Wait for me in the house when you get done. John, take me to Sonya's."

John nodded and Double D got to work. They

began placing the grenades around the outside of the house where they could easily reach them. They had taken the full box that William brought with them and were placing a ton of grenades in the spots they wanted to target. William and John backed down the driveway, on their way to Sonya's house just on the other end of the street.

In pure Sonya fashion, she strolled out of her house as if she had nothing to do but watch out the front window when William and John pulled up. She was all smiles for William.

"Well, howdy stranger! What brings you out this way?" She had her arms open waiting for him to hug her like estranged lovers.

"Hi, Sonya. I'm here to talk to you about the munitions that you gave to Justyn ."

"Why? Is something wrong?" She dropped her arms to her sides. She hated being questioned about stuff and instantly got defensive.

"Whoa," William said with his hands up. "I just want to know how many you used so we know how many were in the box. I'm not here to question their use. I'm sure you had good reason."

"You're damn right I did! I have had a hell of a time out here making sure I had food for these survivors that no one has come for. I lost my husband on a run last week! It's now just me and my boys, and I swear you guys have forgotten about us."

"Ok, Sonya. I'm sorry that you feel like we have forgotten about you. I give you my word I will do better and check in with you. I have just been super busy as we have acquired more areas and now with this recent incident of my son being killed, I'm sorry, but we have been a little busy."

John was standing back at the truck while William met Sonya halfway between the door and the driveway. He could hear everything. He knew she was more upset that he wasn't out here with her as his "matriarch" instead of Tina. John found it hard to keep a straight face so he turned around and acted like he was looking up the road.

Sonya softened, "I'm sorry. I have missed you too, Willy. If I'm being honest, when Sarge and I went out last week, I left him to be eaten by the walkers. I just want you." She started getting closer to William and he grabbed her arms as she tried to wrap them around his waist.

"I need to know, how many grenades were left in that box?" William asked, looking into her eyes.

"There were about six left. I had been using them to keep us from being overwhelmed on runs."

"That's what you have them for. You did nothing wrong, I just needed to know. Now, I'm gonna go talk to John real quick then me and you can go inside for some 'us' time. Ok?" William said quietly to her while pushing her arms down to her sides so she couldn't hug him in front of John. It gave the illusion of secrecy.

Sonya nodded her head and waited by the door. William walked over to John, told him what had transpired, and said he was gonna take care of this woman. John thought about it, that could mean two things and neither was his business. He got in the truck and drove off back toward Nick and Jenn's house. William wrapped his arm around Sonya's shoulders and they walked inside the house together.

13.

Royerson Food Mart was untouched. We walked in and immediately were sickened by the rotting food smell. Moldy, rotten fruits and vegetables as well as the smell of rotten meat made our stomachs roll. Jason had an amazing idea though. He suggested we all go get some Vick's and put it under our noses as crime scene investigators do. We were running to the aisles in front of the pharmacy, ripping open the boxes and slathering the cooling gel under our noses. No one wanted to be the first to throw up.

Once the smell situation had been taken care of, we could focus on the food situation. We walked back to the front and grabbed carts. The store was our playground and we ran through it like we were kids in a candy shop. Jason must have forgotten if he locked the front door because he went back to it about four times. Maybe he was looking out, I'm not sure, but he touched the lock all four times. I just happened to be in the line of sight when he did it. 'OCD havin' mug' was all I could think each time I saw him as I chuckled to myself and shook my head.

Now, I'm not sure how much you watch movies but I am a movie buff. Picture that one scene in the movie when the people were running and having fun in the grocery store as they were also running from zombies, that was us. I think the movie was something like 28-something. You know the movie. It had Cillian Murphey in it and he woke up in a hospital all naked on the hospital bed. No blankets. That shocked the shit out of me. Anyway, how they were running around in a store that was fully stocked, that's how we were except we didn't have fresh fruit to eat. It had been too long. We were having such a good time that we weren't even paying attention to the front. As we were bagging all the food and medicines, we realized that the bass we heard was pounding. Pounding on the windows. We looked at each other and then turned around to look at the front. We should have just stayed blissfully ignorant. We were surrounded.

We had parked farther away than normal which didn't screw us exactly. We were screwed because the walkers were right up at the windows and doors. One of them must have seen us and rang the dinner bell. The walkers looked like they had been rotting in this town for a while. They looked emaciated and dry if you can imagine that. Usually, they are juicy and gross but these have been in this state for the entire six months of this apocalypse.

"Well," Jason started.

"We know. Get comfortable." Jana finished. We finished bagging what we had and found spots where we would be comfortable out of sight of the zombies so we could leave. In all honesty, I liked the fact that we had to take a break because I realized that I forgot a lot of things as I was shopping around so I had time to grab them. I'm young, what can I say?

After what felt like weeks, in reality it was a few hours, and it started getting dark outside, the banging stopped but when I decided to try to peek around the corner, I saw the parking lot, what I could see of it, was full of walkers. I was able to whisper-yell to Jana what I saw and she was able to pass on the message. We all crawled to the back of Royerson's and sat in a circle like children planning some mischief.

"The parking lot looks packed from where I can see," I had said, knowing that the message got transferred through the group and just making sure the translation didn't get lost like in that telephone game.

"Oh, that's what was said." I heard 'The praying law is porked'," Jason said, laughing as quietly as he could.

"Yeah," I said while trying to hold back the laughter, "that's why I repeated it."

We all had a good quiet laugh to not attract attention from the 'porkers'.

"OK, so what's the game plan?" Jana said with less of an accent than usual. I hoped she wasn't losing her accent. I loved that about her.

"That's why I wanted to huddle," Jason said with a smile on his face. "We can stay here tonight and wait them out or we can come up with a plan for a decoy."

Stacy cast her vote, "Well, I vote wait. I am not in the mood to try and kill all them walkers. Besides, aren't we meeting the other group here?"

Jana and Freya agreed. That left me and Jason to cast our votes, it really wouldn't matter either way as the ladies had us beat. Even if we wanted to go out, there were more of them since Dan was gone.

"Ok, we stay. Let's make ourselves comfortable and take shifts watching. Who wants the first shift?" Jason asked.

"I'll take it," I said. I wasn't tired and wanted to see if I could get in the back room or store office. "Do we need any meds? I'm not sure if anyone hit up the pharmacy." Everyone looked at each other like they had never heard of such a thing. I was annoyed at all the dumbfounded looks from everyone. "Well, I guess not," I replied after a little while of the back and forth between everyone. "I will go check the place out. Can we think of anything specific that we may need?" Again, with the looks. I think everyone had either gotten more stupid as the trip had gone on or we all just needed a break from the stress.

"Yeah, I didn't even think of it so that's fine. I'm gonna take a nap after I read. Wake me up for the second watch when you get tired and I'll get up," Jana finally answered.

I nodded at her and she crawled over to her area and began setting up a bed as best as she could with the little amount of clothing this place had. It had the local high school printed on some sweatshirts, hoodies, and sweatpants that the store had made up but were now marked down seventy-five percent because they didn't sell this past winter. This was gonna suck.

I made sure to crawl over to where everyone else followed Jana's lead, grabbing the clothing off the single round rack close to the front of the store by the customer service desk, which was right by the entry doors, and consequently, by the windows where the damned walkers were able to see in. I looked out the windows from a crouched position while everyone grabbed some clothing. Jana was nice and grabbed extra to make me a bed. When everyone was finished, I waited there for a while watching the walkers' heads bob past. The windows were only half windows; the bottom half was a brick wall.

I made rounds while the others slept, walking

upright when I got to the back of the store, crouching when I got close to the front. I did this for hours. I saw the horde out front thinning with every five rounds I had made. They wandered off when they got bored, and we were not very entertaining. I looked for a working clock but the one on the wall had stopped at some point and without electricity, the time clock that the employees would punch in and out on was about as useful as a screen door on a submarine.

I was starting to get tired so as promised, I woke Jana to have her watch for as long as she could. She had an analog watch and whisper-yelled, "Dude, it's four in the morning and you're just now waking me up?" I shrugged and moved over to my sleeping area down the aisle from her. She got up and all I remember was closing my eyes.

Morning hit me, right in the face. I found the only place where the sun reached inside the store and down the aisles. I woke to a blinding light when I rolled over. Jason was up and telling everyone to pack up because the horde had moved on and it was time to find a house to set up in and wait for the mystery people that he was talking to. We all began packing and grabbing the last few essentials that we may need for a few days. Jason then called a huddle at the back of the store when we were all packed.

"So, the plan," Jason started, "is to find a house with a pool that looks semi-blue. We don't want one that is full of gross water, we want to try to use this pool for drinking water and bath water. We need some buckets, which I have already found. We also can use the pool water to flush toilets. So, if we can find it, we can have some basic amenities."

Jana and Freya spoke at the same time about showers and using an actual toilet. I was looking forward to that too as I had begun to smell like a garbage dump with a broken sewer line. We grabbed our carts, which were waiting at the front, and Jason said he wanted us to wait while he went out to the truck first to check our blind spots. He would then put his stuff away and stand watch for the next person. He wanted us to go one at a time so we didn't attract attention and so the next person that was done could help him stand watch for the next person. Naturally, he made me go out second, Stacy third, and when she was standing guard, Freya and Jana could come out at the same time. We nodded in agreement and understanding. It was a solid plan, no one could doubt that.

Jason went out with his cart and we closed the doors behind him. We watched, not breathing, and waited for him to get to the truck. He looked both ways in the parking lot and started walking to the truck that had his camper. We froze when he stopped. Suddenly, his head snapped to the right and so did we. There, coming around the corner, were about four walkers. I looked at Stacy and she was looking at me.

"Do we help him?" I asked, really wanting to know what they expected from me.

"If you don't, I will."

"No, I'm going." I grabbed my crowbar and thought to myself, 'I need to get a knife'. Stacy went over to the door and opened it for me.

I was just outside the door when Jason threw his hand back, palm open, which meant, in Jason-ese, that he wanted me to stop. I waited. The walkers were extremely slow here. They looked like the others, very dried out and emaciated like they hadn't eaten in a very long time. I was still unsure about the metabolism of the walkers, how they digested us if they were dead, what eating us did for them, and more. I had questions, but I was the farthest thing from a scientist. I never passed one science class and it now irked me that I never paid attention because I thought I would never use or need it. Boy, was I ever so wrong.

Jason was standing there, eyes wide, looking at the walkers shambling around the corner. I was standing where they couldn't see me at the front doors, the rest of the group were looking at both of us through the safety of the windows inside the store. It felt like a Mexican standoff. Just then, one of them, a male who could have been in his twenties when he was full of life, and blood, began to dart for Jason. I ran out, crowbar at the ready over my right shoulder, Jason was trying to pull his knife but it was getting stuck. I raced up to the walker and smashed its head in, blood and brain matter going every which way. I turned when I was done with that one to face the other three coming my way. I had hillbilly Jack, Big Bertha, his wife, wearing a moo-moo, and a younger female who looked like she could have been their daughter. She was maybe fifteen years old. I didn't want to dispatch the family but I knew that it was us or them. I went for hillbilly Jack first. He was still massive for a guy who looked like he was trying out for the California Raisins. (If you aren't aware of the California Raisins, get some culture, you swine!)

I went for hillbilly Jack and he was also feeling the love, wanting to kiss me. If it were different circumstances, my heart would have melted. HJ, as I lovingly called my new boo, had his arms out in good old zombie fashion. I managed to duck around him, come up behind him, and slam my crowbar into his overripe melon. I felt someone grab me from behind and, sooner than later, I was being pulled backward. I was looking at the sky and saw that Jason had finally gotten the knife from his belt and taken care of Big Bertha who, by the force of her grip, was trying to have a zombie threesome with me.

"Sorry Bertha, this ain't that kind of party," I said as I was fighting with the dead-again's grip. She was not letting go, even in death.

"Thanks for saving my ass back there," Jason said as he helped release Big Bertha's grip from my shirt.

"I wasn't sure if I was gonna be breakfast or if you were," I chortled.

We got his stuff to the rig and he unloaded it as I stood watch. When he was finished, we followed the rest of the plan and got our things into our respective vehicles and traveling homes. We decided to look for a block of houses to clear on a nice street tucked away from other travelers so we could wait for the new group Jason had made friends with. Jason, again, promised me that once we found a home base and cleared it, he and I would go look for accommodations for me. I was looking forward to being in a house again. In my humble opinion, we could stay here forever.

With everyone packed up, we followed our fearless leader out of the parking lot. We had lost a day but we were all in one piece. THAT was what was important. We drove off to the right, out of the parking lot, going down a side street. The place looked like a natural disaster zone. Clothing and trash were strewn about the street. Teddy bears, papers, slippers, and I think that was a moo-moo, were traveling with the wind. We were driving slowly to keep the noise down but the neighborhood looked devoid of any human life. We saw the occasional walker stumble out from between buildings, but I think most of the town was in the huge horde that kept us holed up inside the store overnight.

We came up to a four-way stop, looked right, left, then right again and Jason decided on going right down the residential street that was behind the store.

"The closer we are to the store, the easier it will be to keep food in our stores," Jason reasoned out loud.

We pulled over and Jason checked his rear-view mirrors on the sides to see how close the random walkers were. He told me to stay in the truck, got out and all I heard was a moan, a couple of grunts, then a thud. Jason came back and motioned for me to get out through the closed window on the driver's side. He went down the line of trucks and campers, getting everyone out. We all huddled up between the rear of his camper and the front of Stacy's vehicle with Valkyrie inside. Valkyrie was still pissed at Stacy for leaving her in the car all night and Stacy knew she was gonna have a lot of making up to do once they got into the house.

"Ok gang," Jason started, "we need to stick together and clear out some houses. I wanted to stay as close to the store as possible so we could make short, quick runs if needed. Let's clear this block and attempt to build a fence system around the block so we can feel somewhat safe."

"I saw a hardware store a little ways back," Freya said.

"Good," Jason said, pointing at her, "we will need to pull stuff from there for our wall."

"I'll take point on the first house," Stacy said.

"Ok, good, I will take the rear. When the point from the first house completes the search, the number two will take point on the next house and the point from the prior house will take the back. We need at least eight houses cleared. Five for our group and the other three could be for the newbies. They can divide up however they see fit." Jason was good at making plans and I was amazed. I wanna be just like him when

I grow up.

"I'll take second for Stacy," I volunteered.

Freya was looking scared but she was relieved after she heard Jason say someone goes in with her. She knew absolutely nothing about clearing a house but she also didn't give herself enough credit. She had come a long way since we met her back at the house in Toledo a few months ago. Jana was more than happy to take second and watch Freya's back while they were clearing houses.

The first house was empty, as was the second. The third house only had one walker and that one was outside so I got to end it as I was at the rear when we reached the third house. It seemed that the other homes also only had one or two walkers to dispatch outside of the homes. We cleared all eight houses without incident. We were floating on cloud nine as we all felt like we had a handle on this apocalypse thing. The next thing we needed to master was quick clean-up skills.

The homes were a mess and we decided we would get further if we worked in groups of two. Jason and

Jana got the first home, and Stacy and I worked on the second home. Freya felt safe enough to tackle a home alone but Jason and I took turns checking on her. Freya left items that were too heavy in the house so that when Jason and I would come to check on her, we would move the items out that were too heavy for her. She would help us if the item was an odd shape or super heavy. She wasn't a punk! We had picked which home we were going to stay in and had all the houses cleaned out by nightfall.

14.

Lee and Chris felt like they were driving for a week straight. They were just trying to get away from the people who called themselves The Federation. Lee and Chris had never met until the night they were picked to go out with Justyn , the head asshole's son. Justyn was a chip off the old block. He was meaner than a nest of hornets that were just shaken by a fearless idiot. They had begun introductions once they were away from Justyn . Lee Edwards was a middle-aged man from a small city in Ohio called Mansfield. They were notorious for their old, haunted prison which was also featured in a couple of major motion pictures. Lee was an avid hunter and enjoyed every minute of it. Before the undead started getting up and walking around again, he was married with kids. They were taken quickly while he was at work when the shit hit the fan.

Chris Sernik was from an even smaller town in Pennsylvania called Hermitage. He was a motorcycle lovin' badass who took no shit, except from his wife and daughter, who were his life. They were separated while on a run and he had hoped that they would be at the camp when he was brought there, but he had not seen them. It was difficult to find them since The Federation separated families based on gender.

"I wasn't given a choice. It was either join them or get fed to the zeds. I have been there for a while though. They have fed us and kept us safe for the most part. I was about to give up anyway. My family was gone. I had nothing and I did NOT want to be without my family," Lee explained while he was driving into Indiana.

"I was pissed when I got there and found out that I would never know if they were there because The Federation asshats would have separated us even if we came in together. I was looking for a way to make it over to the women's camp to find them. If I didn't find my girls and did make it out alive, I was gonna try to free everyone. I would still like to try." Chris's face said he meant it. He was determined to find his family. He just wanted answers.

"This is a pretty sweet ride we got from that guy, huh?" Lee said enthusiastically.

"Yeah, we should probably stop and pick up some survival gear and food. Water especially. We need to find a place that hasn't been picked over," Chris said with some urgency. His stomach was growling and he knew they weren't gonna last long. Justyn didn't pack any rations for them. He figured they would be back within two days.

"We need weapons, too," Lee added. "I mean, the melee weapons are great but if we need to unalive things in a large group and farther away, we are screwed."

Just as Lee finished his sentence, a Royerson's Food Mart came into view. Lee looked at Chris, eyebrows raised, as they pulled into the parking lot. There were a couple of zeds in the parking lot stumbling over some re-dead zeds and shopping carts left behind. They, again, looked at each other in astonishment.

"Are we too late?" Lee turned to Chris as he was scoping out the parking lot.

"The doors are still closed. I'm confused. I wonder how long those things have been down in the parking lot." Chris said out loud, but also to himself.

"Should we check?"

Chris had a habit of scratching under his full salt-and-pepper beard when he was thinking. "Yeah, we should still go look."

Lee pulled up closer to the door. The zeds in the parking lot took notice and began to meander their way. Chris opened his door and grabbed the crowbar while Lee took the bat. They made short work of the five or six zeds that were in the parking lot. Winded, they walked over to the front doors of the food mart. Chris had Lee watch his back, and with more force than necessary, he opened the front door.

"Wow, they didn't even lock the door when they left?" Lee asked and Chris ignored him. Chris was more concerned about more zeds inside.

Lee and Chris walked inside and Chris pulled back Lee by his arm to keep him going any further. Chris then used the crowbar to bang, loudly, on the back end of the check-out lanes. They were wood but covered by metal which made a loud thump and a tinny noise when hit. They waited and heard welcome silence. They saw the carts and grabbed one each.

"I think someone has been in here," Chris yelled to Lee who was a couple of aisles over.

"Yeah, looks like whoever it was had to stay here for a bit of time. I found a makeshift bed," Lee responded.

"So did I," Chris said.

The two continued picking the rest of the edible food off the shelves that wouldn't go bad in the heat. It wasn't enough that the apocalypse happened, but it was also turning into one of the hottest summers the Midwest had had along with the highest humidity on the planet. It was probably an overstatement but it was still miserable. All the cold food, frozen food, and fresh veggies and fruits went bad months ago.

The two put all the food into bags, the water was in gallon containers or packaged with other single bottles which made bagging unnecessary. They looked out to make sure they weren't overrun with zeds and then opened the door. They packed the truck with their haul and decided since it was getting dark, they needed to find a place to sleep. They saw the neighborhood behind the store and decided they were going to scope it out. They left out of the parking lot to the right and instead of going right at the stop sign, they went left to that first corner house. Lee backed the big silver truck up to the garage door. The house had two huge bedrooms, both outfitted with queen beds. It was the perfect size for two lone wolves. They cleared it out, cleaned it up, brought all their food inside, and bedded down for the night. They would explore the town tomorrow.

15.

John pulled up to the house where Justyn , the two goons, Dwayne and Devon, and the homeowners, Nick and Jenn were. Double D were waiting outside for John and William. John walked up to them and told them there were only six grenades and they needed to go in and see what was going on. They nodded and turned to go inside. John was grateful that he didn't have to explain William's absence to them; not that it was any of their business, he just didn't want to have to deal with the questions. Everyone knew William was a cheater. What was there to explain?

John followed behind Devon who followed Dwayne inside the house and saw that Justyn had Nick and Jenn tied up to their dining room chairs, but had those chairs sitting in the kitchen. Nick and Jenn had both been hit a few times in their faces as evidenced by the blood dripping from their noses and mouths. Nick looked a little worse than Jenn.

"Oh, look at this Mr. Federali. Your butt buddies came to help beat up a family minding their own business," Jenn said, looking at the new people entering her home with her one good eye. The other was swollen shut and already turning purple. Justyn had started closed-fisted punching her right in her face a while ago and gave her another good strike to the mouth.

"Shut the fuck up, bitch. Unless you're gonna tell me where my brother is, you will only speak when spoken to, you country whore!" Justyn screamed, only centimeters from her face.

Justyn stood up and looked at the other three meandering through the door. Dwayne and Devon were whispering back and forth to each other and chuckling at the damage. "Where's Dad, John?" Justyn replied after looking at the other two chuckleheads.

"He is 'taking care' of Sonya. There were six in the box when you started and she said that was all she had left. Dad said to take care of this situation," John regurgitated what William had told him to do as he leaned on the counter.

"What does that mean? 'Taking care of?'" Justyn

was getting annoyed.

"I'm not sure, I didn't ask and it's none of my business," John said to Justyn .

Justyn turned his fury onto Nick and Jenn. "Last chance. Where is my brother? Who were the people you helped get past Sonya's house?"

Nick tried to talk through two closed eyes, one side of his mouth fattened, and teeth missing, "The people were no one. They were just getting to Nashville. I never saw your brother."

"FINALLY! SOME kind of info I can use," Justyn started walking out of the house. When he noticed the others were not coming, he stopped and yelled, "Do you want to die in the rubble or are you coming?"

That gave the other three the initiative they needed to get moving. They could hear Jenn yelling and banging the chair on the floor. The men presumed she was trying to get free to get her and her husband out of the house before they found out what "rubble" meant, but Justyn was a champ at knots and they were never going to get out of those.

"Ok, so here is the plan," Justyn turned and looked at the crew, "We are going to all throw at least one ready grenade at the house after I throw two into the kitchen. Aim for windows. I want this house to come down."

They waited for Justyn to throw the two live grenades in the kitchen, then they all took their turns, pulling their pins and chucking the grenades into the house. They ran behind the trucks for cover. The initial two exploded, they stood upright to watch Dwayne throw his grenade after pulling the pin. Right through the dining room window, the guys crouched behind the truck. First, there was the crash from the breaking glass, then the third BOOM! They all started laughing as the screams from Nick and Jenn could be heard. The guys stood again and now Devon threw his live grenade and hit the second-story window above the kitchen where the two were yelling and crying. Another large BOOM. They stood from their crouches and heard splintering wood creaking and then falling as a dust and insulation plume came from the kitchen area. Dwayne and Devon were laughing with Justyn and high-fiving each other. John was the last with his grenade. He pulled the pin, yelled "FIRE IN THE HOLE!" and they all ducked again behind the truck. There was the crash of the living room glass then the final BOOM! The noise that came from the multiple explosions was sure to draw every walker in the state. The guys jumped into the trucks and took off to Sonya's house to pick up William. Playtime was over. Justyn got a location out of them and he intended on going to Nashville to find these people who killed his brother.

The men pulled up to Sonya's house and got out of the truck. John hung back because he knew what William and that nasty woman were doing. He wasn't gonna get in trouble with William for interrupting his adult playtime. Justyn went up to the house and just walked in. John waited at the truck and was not disappointed. William came storming out of the house with Justyn and Double D following.

"John, take me home. NOW," William yelled at John, stomping to the truck. John got in the driver's seat while William climbed into the passenger's seat and the other three jumped in the back of the crew cab.

The drive back home was quiet and the high tension could be cut with a knife. When the men finally got home, Justyn told William that he was showering, packing for a couple of days, and then going back out. He needed to get to Nashville to avenge his brother.

William dropped his heavy hand on Justyn 's shoulder, "Son, I'm damned proud of you for taking this so seriously. Leave no witnesses and take no prisoners. Make me proud son. The torch will be passed to you and I need to go to The Federation with some type of news. We can't have these people ruin what we started. We will run this country, son. You will be in the Presidential seat if we play our cards right."

"I won't let you down, Dad." That was all Justyn could get out. He went inside, said hi to his mother, and showered.

Tina saw William come in, and with tears in her eyes, she asked, "What do you have my son doing now? Where is Robert? I thought you were going to get him."

"Tina, you need to sit down."

"Don't patronize me. Just tell me what the fuck is

going on and where my boy is. Why did you come home without him?"

"Robert was found dead about twenty minutes south of Findlay in a small town called Arlington. He was shot. After talking to the people who let the survivors escape in McComb, we found out where they were headed and we believe that these people are the ones that killed our son. Justyn is going out after packing to make them pay for killing Robert."

Tina crumpled. William caught her before she fell to the floor. He held her and she had a vice grip on him. She cried for a while, mourning her lost son that she didn't get to say goodbye to. John walked in and his heart broke. There was so much death, so much loss. He was tired of the loss.

Justyn came out and was ready to go. He saw his mom being held by his dad. "Mom, I got this. I am gonna make them pay!"

Tina turned to look at her only son. "You better. He was a good boy. Kill them all," she said with venom in her voice and a little spittle escaping her clenched teeth.

Justyn nodded his understanding and went outside. He almost ran into John when he went out. John looked at him, "I want to go with you. I want to avenge Robert. He was my best friend. These people need to pay and you need backup if there are more than just a couple of them."

Justyn looked at him and nodded. He knew that John was right and he knew that he could trust John to have his back. "You're right. I will need help, and the other two Dad made me bring hit me in the head and took off in one of our trucks. I know I can trust you. You have been with us since the beginning. Go pack a few days' worth of food and clothing, I will be waiting for you in the truck." John took off to the house to get packed.

16.

Lee and Chris got up with the sun. It was the first time they had got to sleep in actual beds, inside a house, without a mud floor or the smell of raw sewage in the air in six months. They went to the kitchen to make a plan for the day. It was an exploring day and they needed a game plan.

"I think we need to check out the neighborhood first. We then should see if we can find a hardware store to fortify the doors and windows. Then we can see if we can build a wall to keep people from entering the neighborhood. I want to first see if there are any survivors that we may have to include in building the gate at the front of the neighborhood. Have you ever lived in a gated community?" Lee looked at Chris with a huge smile on his face.

Chris chuckled, "No, I haven't. I also have never had to run for my life. We also need to hit up any sporting goods stores so we can get guns and ammo. They should have some smaller caliber weapons, ammo, other types of survival gear, and bows and arrows. It wouldn't hurt to grab more bats either."

"Yeah! Great idea. Are we walking around the neighborhood or should we drive?"

"I think we should start small and walk up and down this street today. We need to clear each house and make sure the dead aren't lying in wait for us inside houses." Chris didn't sound so sure about his opinion.

"No, I think that's a great idea. We need to start small. I'm the type that gets all excited about stuff and tries to do too much. I need someone like you to keep me in line," Lee said, grateful that Chris was with him.

"Ok then. Let's get moving so we can be back here to go to the sporting goods store by lunch. It's been hot lately," Chris said, grabbing his bat. He wanted to hurry up and get to the store so he could get some survivalist supplies. In his mind, Lee was a giant kid. He may have been in his forties but he acted like an overgrown teenager with just enough knowledge to make him dangerous.

Jason was out in front of the homes they cleared

checking them out. He was making mental notes for the fortification of each house just in case they had to fight to keep their homes. The random guy that Stacy knew, who was also part of the redneck group back in Toledo, had found them. He wasn't the brightest guy from the looks of it and now he was a dead dummy after getting shot. Jason had a bad feeling that the death of that guy would haunt them and it wouldn't be pretty. His asshole was at a number ten pucker.

Lee and Chris left the house and began walking across the entry street into the neighborhood. They could see the parking lot of Royerson's Food Mart from where they were. There were a couple of houses on the short drive between the parking lot and the corner of the next street that they were on. Lee looked over to the parking lot on his right, looked down the street the other way to his left, and then straight ahead. That's what made him jump and pee a little. He saw someone walking on the sidewalk looking at the houses as if he were evaluating the house for a repair of some sort. The guy wasn't huge but he wasn't a small guy and he didn't walk like a zed. Lee was confused.

Chris walked up to him, gave Lee another little

jump, and looked at what Lee was looking at. Chris almost had a heart attack right where he stood. Lee's mouth was open and he rubbed his eyes. Chris had the same look.

"Am I seeing things or is that guy acting like the end of the world was just a minor inconvenience in his remodel plans?" Lee said quietly to Chris.

"I'm seeing this too. Do we approach him or work around him?" Chris asked without taking his eyes off him.

"I mean, the whole point was to find survivors, and look, we found one."

"All you had to do was say, 'Yes, Chris. We should go talk to him.' You dickhead."

Lee and Chris started walking towards Jason. They made it across the street and up to the neighboring house to Jason. Jason saw movement out of the corner of his eye and spun to face them with his handgun pointed in their direction. They stopped; hands shot up in the air almost immediately.

"Whoa, buddy!" Chris said, "We don't mean you

any harm. We just pulled in here last night down at the corner house. Do you live here?"

"I do now. I'm Jason. Who are you?" Jason asked as he holstered his firearm.

"This is Chris and I'm Lee," Lee said. Chris thought he was acting like a kid who just started school for the year and met new friends. It made him chuckle at how free Lee was.

"Well, nice to meet you boys," Jason said, offering his hand to shake. "You said you're at the house on the corner right? I didn't think anyone else was here."

"Really, neither did we," Chris answered. "Yeah, we took over the house on the corner late last night. We got a few supplies from the store over there, and after we cleared the house, we thought we would stay for a while. Whatever you do, do NOT go to northern Ohio."

Jason froze. "Why?"

"We just came from that way. We were prisoners in a camp full of survivors. These people lied to us and offered us 'safety' but then when we got there, they told us we had to help them or get fed to the zeds," Lee rambled on about the conditions at the camp. As he was doing that, Freya came out of her house next door with Stacy.

Freya came up to the three men as Lee was talking about the camp and she went ghost white. Jason and Stacy saw the change in her body language and asked her if she was okay.

"You guys came from that camp in Ohio?" She looked at Lee with wide eyes.

"Yeah," Lee looked at her with concern.

"I also came from there. How did you get away? They have that place on lockdown."

Lee and Chris looked at each other. Chris started, "It wasn't easy. We had to wait for the right moment. We thought we were gonna die in that camp and along comes the head honcho's son, Justyn . He picked me and Lee to go with him on a mission looking for his brother. We ended up finding his brother dead in Arlington. While we were there, I took my shot. I hit him over the head, knocked him out and we took the truck and left him there for the zeds to get."

Now Stacy, Jason, and Freya, with tears in her eyes, all looked at each other. Jason put his finger to his lips to keep the girls from talking and looked at the two men, "We should go inside and talk." Jason showed them to his front door and let them in. Freya and Stacy went and got Jana and me.

"What the fuck, Stacy? The first comfortable bed I have been in since we left Toledo and now 'the master' has summoned us to his castle! Who let you in?" I asked after being woken up. I hate being woken up and that makes me a very cranky boy, especially if I wasn't ready to get up.

"Hey, you little shit, get the fuck up. We found people and they are from the redneck camp back in Ohio. Get over to Jason's now," Stacy yelled at me while managing to tear through my room and get me clothes to get dressed. It figured the first time I had a spot of my own in months and I got woken up for some bullshit meeting. I begrudgingly got up and dressed, and then made my way over to Jason's place.

I walked through the front door without knocking

and heard voices coming from the kitchen.

"...they walked up to me while I was outside looking at how I could fortify the houses. This is Lee, and this is Chris. They came from the hillbilly camp. Remember them?" Jason was introducing new people to everyone. I was even less happy than when I woke up.

I slowly start walking to the kitchen and see everyone shaking the hands of one tall and one shorter middle-aged guy who must be Lee and Chris.

"Glad you could make it, Aaron," Jason said to me in a half-scolding and half-joking manner.

I gave Jason a quick smile and turned to the two men, reaching out my hand to them. "Forgive me, fellas. I was sleeping. Good to meet ya. I'm Aaron and yes, I'm young but this fine fella," I said, putting my hand out toward Jason after shaking the hands of the newcomers, "he has taught me a lot." Gotta give props where they were due, even if he was an asshole that morning.

"We are so happy to have met you guys," Lee said.

"We do have some disturbing news for you though. I can tell you that the head honchos back at the camp are looking for you all."

This made everyone freeze in place. All eyes were on Lee waiting for him to continue.

"Well, let's have a seat. Are you hungry?" Jason asked as everyone sat.

"I can get some Pop-Tarts or something else if you are," Stacy interjected.

"Yeah, let's eat and then talk," Lee thought twice about what he just said. "Unless you want to hear it. I just didn't want to ruin your breakfast."

Jason looked around and read the room, "I think we should hear it now. We are pretty sure we already know what this is about. Stacy, if you don't mind getting the stuff from the cupboard."

"Nope, I'm on it. Lee, spill the beans. I can hear you while I'm getting things together."

Lee went on about how he and Chris got this far. He started at the camp where Justyn picked the two of them from the whole group and ended the story with what they were doing outside this morning. Chris interjected when he felt Lee was leaving out important information or when he felt he needed to clarify that they were not like those people. The story was so engaging that everyone forgot there was food on the table. Freya looked relieved when she found out that the camp didn't even recognize that she and Dan had left. Not that it mattered anymore as Dan had been killed by Robert which is why he met the end that he did.

My palms were sweating and I'm sure I looked guilty as Jason looked at me. Jason decided to say, "Yes. We did kill Robert. He killed one of our own. We had no idea why he came after us. We were stopped, fixing a blown tire on one of our vehicles, when he showed up. Stacy knew him."

Stacy interrupted, "I know the whole family and what they are about. They are all no good."

"We know," Chris said, "that's why I hit him over the head with the bat and knocked him out cold. I don't know how long he was down and I'm not sure if he was bitten, but I do know that he will be looking for us as well, if he's alive. He has connections in McComb and they saw you guys leave the area and know that a couple helped ya from up the street."

Jason kept his cool, I did not. "Nick and Jenn?" I started shaking. Just the thought that we may have gotten them beat up or worse, all because we never were caught by their sadistic crew.

"I think that was their names but I can't be sure. I only saw the woman who was the snitch," Chris said.

The conversation continued but I was in my little world trying to figure out how we managed to piss people off just by leaving the area. This was not good. I knew what happened when you pissed off the neighborhood kingpin. They have PhDs in making your life miserable. Lee interrupted my thought process by wanting to know if we would be interested in building a gate.

"Chris and I think it's a good idea for us to build a gate and fortify some homes inside a fence. We would need your help if you all are willing," Lee was looking for an answer right at that moment and Jason's brows raised.

"Well," Jason stated as he adjusted his position in the world's most uncomfortable chair, "we weren't planning on staying that long. We are only here to meet up with a group, but then leave for Nashville. You guys should think about coming with us." There it was, the phrase I was waiting for. We said, way back at the house, how we weren't taking in strangers anymore and we ended up with a dog, a new group that we only spoke with over the radio, and now these two.

I had to speak up, "I mean, the road will be rough. We will have to get a few more campers and RVs as well as go on supply runs to stock the RVs. Do we have that kind of time?" I was trying to give the two a way out as well as give us the option to rethink taking in strangers.

Chris answered me, "We have nothing now so following you guys to Nashville works well for us. I may be able to find my family there. That's how I came to be in the camp back in Ohio. I was looking for my wife and daughter. I never found them, so Nashville is the next best place to look." Tears began to well in the older man's eyes and I knew at that moment, I was the asshole.

"It's settled then," Jason started getting up out of the chair that he couldn't stand to sit in any longer, "we will fortify the street. We will build a fence around our four houses on this side of the intersection, then another four houses in their direction. It will only be sixteen houses in total with four on each side of the street. We should use as many natural barriers as possible. When I say natural barriers, I mean vehicles, houses, and current fences in yards. Things already in the area. We can build up the fences and use the vehicles as the bottom layer of our fence and maybe even as a gate at the front. Do you guys have any ideas?"

I had to admit that Jason knew what he was doing. The two newcomers and Jason began planning. Chris and Lee told Jason about the hardware stores they knew about. Jason told them about the setup that we had back home and they loved it and wanted to do the same.

"Oh my God, if we could have cold beers and hot showers again, I will kiss you right on the mouth," Lee said to Jason. Jason laughed a little and then looked over at Stacy and gave her a look that said "I still got it". Stacy rolled her eyes.

Stacy interrupted the newly forming bromance, "We can show you how to make the house more comfortable. You can keep your kisses."

Jason got ready with the two new guys to go out on a run. Chris got the keys to one of our other trucks, Lee went and got the keys from the house as well as their truck and drove it to the house, and Jason got his truck ready to go. They left me behind. I saw that Stacy had started cleaning up the kitchen in Jason's house so I got up off the chair and noticed Jana and Freya doing their own thing. I decided I was going to go back to my house and go back to sleep.

"I'm going back to the house and going back to bed. Have them wake me when it's time for me to help," I said as I left. I could feel their eyes boring a hole in my back as I left. I think I just needed to go back to sleep. I was just annoyed from the moment I opened my eyes. I was starting to get that sick and tired feeling I had gotten when I was in a foster home too long. My mind started to make up scenarios that would make me even more mad at the group. I shook my head as I walked into my temporary housing situation. I needed to not have those thoughts. Once they started, they spiraled out of control.

I was gently shaken awake by Jana. "Aaron, Jason is looking for you. Aaron." She was being nice about waking me.

I rubbed my eyes, "How long have I been sleeping?"

"You have only been sleeping for a couple of hours. I think that all this being on the run, sleeping in the campers, and the constant adrenaline dumps have caught up with you. Jason and the other two are back and want you to help. You did say to wake you, so I thought I would come over and do it since I know how angry Stacy has been lately. I think there is a problem with Valkyrie, and Stacy isn't handling it well. I haven't seen much of the dog." Jana was making small talk as I woke up.

"Thanks, Jana. I appreciate you. I'm up, you can let them know I'll be down in a few."

"Ok, honey. See ya soon." Jana turned and left. She has always been my favorite human. She's so real and still tries to be kind.

I got dressed and left the house to walk across the street to where Jason and the other two men were removing two-by-fours and metal sheets. They had also grabbed prefabricated fencing panels that they found at Lowes or a Home Depot. Since they were just displays, there were not many in stock. I immediately fell in line, removing items from the backs of the trucks and stacking where the guys had everything staged. We got everything out a lot quicker with just one more set of hands. The girls were inside making us lunch as we were working. Freya made this amazing lemonade that had a sprig of mint in it. It was so refreshing that I wanted to just bathe in it. After lunch, we got started building the perimeter fence. We decided to save the gate for last. Every once in a while we would have to take care of a stray walker but thankfully, no major hordes.

The dark was creeping in and we had gotten all the posts set. We wanted to move as many of the cars around as possible to use them as a bottom barrier. We would then put the metal sheets on top of them, fastening them to the wood poles. The parts that were on the roof of the cars would be secured with ninety-degree elbow hardware to stabilize the metal sheets and make it less likely that the dead would be able to wiggle them loose.

"What about the openings at the hood and trunk? There will be a gap that either people or walkers could get through." I asked. Of course, Jason already thought of that.

Jason looked at me with a smile and just simply said, "Chicken wire." He kept it moving, wanting to get as much done as possible before it was dark. We got quite a few cars moved in place before it was too dark to see. We called it quits and went into Jason's house to eat the dinner the ladies prepared.

Jason, Chris, and Lee had remembered to get generators. To my surprise, the girls had hooked up the generators and even set up the solar panels that came with them. We had cold fridges, central air, and hot water in no time!

17.

Justyn was staring off into space when John came out to the truck. It made John nervous. He had never seen the family this angry. They were all loose cannons and he had wondered if he was going to make it through this thing or if he would die next to one of these idiots. John put that all behind him as he climbed into the passenger side of the truck. It wasn't every day that he was not driving. The passenger seat felt foreign to him.

Justyn took off from the base camp driving south. IIe had the look of a man who had just been through the ringer. John leaned on the passenger door with the understanding that this was going to be one of the longest rides of his life. John closed his eyes and went to sleep.

John was jolted awake by the shaking. "Hey, pissant, get up. I need your help." John opened his groggy eyes and saw Justyn leaning over him.

"What? Where are we?" John said, trying to rub exhaustion from his eyes.

"We can't get through. I need you to help me clear this horde." Justyn said as he smacked the back of John's head.

"SHIT! STOP!" John yelled, forgetting that Justyn said the word *horde*. He stopped and looked up to see about twelve undead in front of the truck. They were far enough away up the street that they could get out and get ready, but John's outburst had taken away their stealth advantage.

"Nice, dickhead. They know we are here now." Justyn got out of the truck and held his bat at the ready.

John got out holding the crowbar he had found in the back seat and holding his nose. "Oh. My. God. Do they stink more than usual?"

"It's pretty bad. I'm not sure why they smell so bad. I don't think our holding cells smell this bad," Justyn answered.

As if on cue, a huge, muscle-bound, eight-foot-tall giant undead...THING...came out of the woods off to the left of the state route they were using to travel.

"What in the actual FUCK is that?" Justyn asked, losing focus on the horde in front of him.

John was in shock at the size of this new beast he had never seen before on a road he had traveled many times in the last week. This thing had patchy brown hair on its head, a shiny scalp where there was no hair, and bright blue eyes that could be seen from miles away. He had the biggest muscles the two men had ever seen, it would have made a bodybuilder jealous, and unfortunately for the pair of ordinary, alive humans, the giant was naked. His willy waved and bounced with each step the giant took. His body, overall, looked greasy and slick with some strange substance.

"It's him that smells so bad," John suggested, not knowing the answer but only assuming that the massive being was responsible for the offensive odor.

"Who cares WHO it is," Justyn yelled back to him as he set himself to swing on the first walker he came to. "Just start killing these things!"

John walked away from the safety of the truck and into the dwindling horde. John was not a front-line guy. He was more than happy being the lowly driver. The one who wasn't in charge of anything. Yet, here he was, swinging the crowbar like a professional baseball player. John hated that he had now been promoted to enforcer. He had seen how things had ended with this family and others they had put their trust in. Now with his best friend gone, it was going to end badly for him.

Justyn was swinging the bat like a home run derby contestant and hitting his mark each time. Black ooze was flying everywhere and John even got hit a couple of times by the spatter. He made sure he was careful not to get it in his mouth or eyes, he didn't want to find out if that was another way people could turn. He thought he would try it on the survivors that he had helped bring in though. Once he got back to the compound, that is. He couldn't exactly test it right now. He and Justyn were almost done clearing the walkers when all of a sudden, there was a roar that was never heard by them before. They had made a fatal error, they forgot about the giant walker.

John looked for Justyn who had finished disposing of the last walker. Justyn had cleared most of them and was now huffing and puffing like he had run a marathon. No doubt his arms felt like wet, useless noodles. John was surprised he still held onto his bat. Justyn and John were looking at the giant and vice versa. The giant roared again but was walking toward them as if he were a toddler just learning to walk. John and Justyn found it mildly comical but they did need a gameplan to bring down the giant undead.

" Justyn , how are we gonna do this without getting hurt?" John asked, trying his hardest to not sound like a bitch.

"I'm not sure because I'm beat. Just aim for his head is all I can say." Justyn was still breathing heavily and John was concerned that he wouldn't be able to recover.

The eight-foot behemoth waddled, unsurely, out to the street they were standing on from the woods off to the left of them. The two men stood at the ready, hoping that the giant wouldn't learn how to run. He, again, let out a roar that the men could feel in their chest cavities. John anxiously looked at Justyn and saw Justyn had steeled himself for the fight that was about to ensue. John took note that Justyn was still breathing heavily, but not as heavily as before. John also noticed that his breathing had increased to almost hyperventilating. John attempted to slow his breaths down but his nervous system would not allow it. He was now in fight or flight mode and had zero control. Whoever was driving the anxiety bus was in charge now.

Slowly and wobbly, the giant got closer. He had the look of hunger in his eyes and did not want to miss out on his little snack. Only God knew how many calories this thing needed to eat just to keep walking around, but he was sure it was even more hungry than the normal size walkers. The giant was within striking distance, for the giant that was. He lifted a heavy arm and attempted to swing it at the two men standing in the street. Justyn dropped to the street and John jumped backward, trying to dodge the log-size arm.

Justyn quickly got up and swung the bat at the head of the giant as it completed the follow-through. Justyn connected with the giant's nose; it made a nasty crunching sound to let the men know that he had connected. What Justyn hadn't anticipated was the giant bringing his arm back the way it had come and in turn, the upper arm of the giant connected with Justyn 's abdomen, sending not only the air out of Justyn 's lungs but also sending him back about ten feet from where he was standing, leaving John all alone when the giant stood up straight. John pissed himself right there.

John didn't see Justyn get up and he knew it was up to him and his crowbar to take out this monster or be one of the monster's minions. He didn't think The Federation thought that this could have happened when they set off the infection. There was a lot they didn't think was going to come to fruition when they devised this plan. Now he is about to be lunch to one of The Federation's monsters that they aren't even aware exists.

The giant and John made eye contact. The bright blue eyes of the beast bore right into John and he felt like he was going to now shit himself since he had already pissed himself. The giant had focused all his attention on John and John wanted to move but found that he couldn't. He was stuck, looking into the eyes of the giant. The giant grabbed John around his neck and began to squeeze. John dropped his crowbar and attempted, in vain, to unhinge the single monstrous hand around his neck. The giant was beginning to lift John off the ground and John began kicking as the pressure on his neck made his head feel like a zit about to be popped.

Justyn was finally getting up from where he landed, John saw him out of the corner of his eye before the dark started coming into his vision from lack of oxygen. Justyn was yelling something, but John couldn't hear him. John only heard his heartbeat in his ears and it was racing. John's last thought was not of any girls, food, or his family. His last thought was, 'Look at the teeth on this thing'. John's body could no longer handle the pressure and the last thing that Justyn saw as he was running to free his friend was John's eyes pop out of his head, followed by blood and brains, his mouth popped open like a jack-in-the-box and his tongue lolled, along with his ears oozing blood. The monster, who couldn't have been more pleased with his handy work, smiled, and began to lick up all the escaping blood and brain matter like John was a push-pop, right before the massive beast bit into his face.

18.

After a few days of waiting for the other group to meet us at the supermarket, we were beginning to lose hope that they would be coming at all. Jason was outside at least three times a day trying to get a hold of the new group that was supposed to be meeting us. One day, Jason finally did get a response, but it wasn't what he was looking for. I was standing out there with him, looking around, making sure our defenses held, while Jason was on the radio.

"Indiana Group, do you copy?" Jason spoke into the radio. He was standing out in the yard of his house at dusk, in his usual spot in the apron of the driveway while trying to raise the other group to find out if they were still coming, if they needed help, or whatever else he could find out.

"Yeah, who's this?" a male responded.

Jason got all excited and looked at me wide-eyed, quietly questioning why the person on the other end didn't know who he was. "You know who this is! I have been talking to you for the last week or more. It's Jason." Shaking his head as he replied.

"No, I don't know you but I would like to. Where are you?" the unknown male asked in reply.

"We are waiting for your group in Greensburg. We are in the neighborhood right behind Royerson's Supermarket. We told you that we would..." Jason stopped and it hit him that maybe the male, Bobby, that he had been conversing with prior was possibly injured or dead. "Where is Bobby?"

"Bobby ain't here right now. I'm Justyn , his right hand. I remember him saying something to me about y'all. I will be there in less than twenty-four hours."

I whipped my head around when he said his name. "Isn't that..." was all I could get out before Jason finally caught on that the man he was speaking to was looking for them. Jason had just told him where to find us.

"Ok, Justyn ," trying to play it off like he didn't just realize who Justyn was. "Is Bobby ok? I also can talk to Mary."

"Nah, Mary ain't available either," Justyn said

with a slight smile. That was when Jason knew they were all dead.

"Well, we are going to move on. We can't wait for your group anymore. We will see you at the safehouse in Charleston." Jason attempted to throw off the man on the other end of the radio.

"If there was one in Charleston. Good try, though. I know you're just tryin' to throw me off your trail. I'll see you soon buddy," Justyn left the air dead.

"SHIT!" Jason and I both said to each other. We quickly walked up to the house to tell the others that we needed to leave.

The front door of Jason's house flew open, scaring the group. They were all huddled around Valkyrie who had made a recovery from whatever illness she had. Valkyrie was making her rounds and letting everyone pet her and her, in return, giving kisses to each person. Jason didn't pay any attention to Valkyrie as she walked up to his hand and gave it a little quick lick.

"Guys, that group of rednecks knows where we are, I just tried to call Bobby, some guy got on and said his name was ' Justyn ' and he was less than a day's travel from us. I was an idiot and he baited me to tell him where we were...I can't believe I was that stupid!" Jason began smacking himself on the head and I just stood there looking at him like he had three heads. I turned and looked at the group who was staring at us.

"We have to go now. We don't know where this guy is or how many people are with him," I spoke and that's when they all started moving.

Lee and Chris went to stand watch at the gate. There was never anything more than walkers but they were the closest to the gate and one could get their stuff together while the other watched then switch out. Since fresh meat was standing at the gate and they could smell it, the walkers started banging on the metal gate that we had made. That ended up bringing more to the front.

Everyone grabbed their important things and met in the street. Vehicles were lined up after they were packed and we made our way to the gate. The pounding was so loud we had to yell to hear each other. Lee and Chris were in charge of the gate because they volunteered. They had their truck sitting off to the side running inside the gate. They would open the gate, fight them off so we could all get out and when the horde was thinned, one would jump in the truck and pull it out of the area just past the gate while the other closed the gate and jumped in the running truck so they could meet us at the supermarket parking lot and then take off as a group to Nashville.

I was thrilled that it was going well. Lee and Chris were expert zombie hunters, smacking the daylights out of the undead devils. Jason passed first, Freya and Jana second, Stacy third, and I brought up the rear like I always do. I was passing Chris who was on my left when I saw that he was so badly outnumbered that he wasn't going to make it if he didn't have help. I pulled off to the side and kept my truck running, jumping out to help, but I was not in time. Chris had been overrun by a huge horde of walkers. We weren't sure where they came from because there were not that many at the front gate all week.

I saw a huge three-hundred-pound lady in a sunflower moo-moo take a hefty chunk out of his right shoulder. He screamed as he went down on his belly and that made Lee stop and look at him. Lee was then taken down by a wiry teenage male walker who was super-fast. This kid must have been into Parkour before he got bitten because he was jumping off things and over things like I have only seen done on extreme sports shows. The teen took Lee to the ground as did another huge woman who was waddling up. The huge woman fell on top of Chris and pinned him to the ground. Their screams were the only dinner bell the other walkers needed as they all went over to the two piles, fell to the ground, and began to dig in. I was taken aback by what I was looking at. I almost became dinner for a slow walker who looked so emaciated that he must have been low on the food chain of zombies.

Stacy came running from behind with Valkyrie and scared the shit out of me. I turned to look at her and saw her mouth moving. Why I couldn't hear her was a mystery to me, so I furrowed my brow and tilted my head, looking at her like she was speaking a foreign language. After a few seconds and a lick, followed by a whine from Valkyrie, my ears finally picked up that she was telling me to get back in the truck, someone was in the grocery store parking lot and it was probably Justyn . I shook off the shock and got back in my vehicle. We were trying to escape, but Justyn had started shooting our vehicles from the middle of the street. How had he gotten here so quickly? I answered my question in my head, 'Because he lied about his location, idiot!'

Shotgun noises rang out amongst the quiet and that made the walkers start coming our way. The emaciated walker kept his eyes on me and did not change direction. The walkers that were not chewing on my two new friends started walking toward the noise. I had to reach back into the truck to grab my bat before the emaciated walker, or any other that may have been walking by, took a chunk out of me. The last thing I wanted was to become one of them. I am not cut out for all that walking! I grabbed the bat just in time. I smelled it before I saw the open rotten maw of the walker trying to make me a very long-awaited dinner. Pushing him back a bit before I clobbered him on the head, I then went and began fighting the horde with my friends. We prayed that we missed the bullet spray from the shotgun that Justyn was aiming in our direction.

I managed to stop fighting long enough to see that Justyn was at the end of the street, shooting in our direction. Not to help us, but shooting at us. I could not believe that he had found us and I was pissed at Jason for leading him right to us. I knew it wasn't his fault. I knew that I would have done the same thing if I were him in that situation. The only difference is Jason, our security guru, got complacent. He had gotten out of the security mindset and let the momentary security that we did have fool him into thinking that we were far enough away that he didn't have to worry about The Federation. I feared that Lee and Chris were not going to be the only losses of the day.

A yell woke me up from my inner monologue and I witnessed Jason take a shotgun hit. Stacy screamed and Valkyrie began viciously growling and barking. I had to walk around the vehicles to see a huge female walker trying to take a bite out of Stacy and Valkyrie trying to pull the rather large woman off of Stacy. 'Do they only have three-hundred-pound women in this town?' I pondered as I began running over to Stacy. Jana was closer to Stacy and was already trying to get the huge woman off her.

Standing over them, I yelled, "Stacy, close your eyes and mouth!" I gave her a second, Jana took a few steps back, then swung the bat knocking off the head of the obese woman and sending it rolling up the street toward Justyn . Stacy was covered in gore from the huge beast. Thankfully that was the second to last monster we needed to put down. The very last was Justyn , who must have been out of ammo at that time as I hadn't heard a peep from anyone but Stacy and Jason. I looked toward the end of the street where he was standing and he was no longer there. He and his truck were gone out of the parking lot. I left Stacy to get up off the ground with Jana's help as she didn't seem hurt and went over to Jason who was snuggled in between two of our vehicles.

"Hey bro, you good?" I asked as I knelt to assess the damage. He was shot in the shoulder and the side as far as I could see from the blood that had been soaked up by his shirt.

"Yeah, it felt like I had gotten bitten by something then I couldn't use my left arm. I didn't feel it till a few seconds after that." He was scrunching his face in pain with his eyes closed.

"You want the good news or the bad news first?" I asked as I looked under his shirt at his wounds, helping him to sit forward a bit.

"Bad, I guess," Jason replied.

"The hole in your shoulder is through and through which is good, I'm not sure of the damage inside which is bad," I said.

"Well, what's the good?"

"The good news is your side is just a graze! You will live, and honestly, I'm not sure if that's good or bad for you. It's good for the group though," I said with a smile, gently leaning him back against the rear bumper of his truck.

"Fuck," Jason exclaimed. "We need to get moving, too. Can you just bandage me up?"

"Yeah, that's what I was gonna do anyways." I left him sitting there while I went and got the first aid kit.

Freya, Jana, and Stacy, covered in gore, walked up to where I was sitting with Jason and kept him company while I went into Jason's camper to get the kit. While inside, I grabbed a couple of towels and wet them for the girls to wash off some of the gore they had on them.

I handed the wet hand towels to the ladies and they smiled like I had just given them pie. I bent down to help Jason pull off his shirt so I could bandage up his wounds. After bandaging his wounds and the girls had mostly cleaned off, we pulled Jason to his feet and began surveying the area. Lee and Chris began to reanimate so I went over and clubbed them both in their heads to keep them from getting up and becoming a problem.

Stacy cleaned off Valkyrie as I was walking back to the group and I saw she had tears in her eyes. Freya and Jana were also crying quietly for the loss of our new friends who, let's be honest, just saved our bacon. Freya and Jana were helping Jason get into his camper. Freya volunteered to drive my truck that we had gotten while out on a run one of the days that we had been in the neighborhood. It was all starting to run together because it felt like it was the same thing every day. Running for our lives, fighting humans trying to kill us, fighting the undead, settling down in a place, getting comfortable, having it ripped out from under us, then leaving, just to start over again. I was thinking that we had left behind so many generators and gas cans that it felt like we were just terraforming for survivors.

I am completely over this apocalypse. At first, I was excited! No cops, no one was gonna tell me what to do. Now, I'm done. We have lost a lot in the last few months and summer is almost over. We needed to get moving to Nashville so we could get into a community and we wouldn't have to do it all ourselves. At this rate, we would be homeless and without supplies for the winter, and in this area, winter is not nice.

Freya, Jana, and I huddled up around the map. We plotted our course and decided that the only way that we could be safe with Jason being out of the game, was a straight shot to Nashville. We had to get there. It was our only hope to find a doctor and make sure Jason survived this wound and could use his arm when it healed.

"Where is Stacy?" Jana said, looking around while the rest of us were looking at the map.

"I'm sure she's cleaning up. She had a lot of nasty on her," I responded to Jana and that seemed to bring everyone back to the map.

"I guess we should get some rest. Jason can't be moved and I know after that fight, we are all exhausted. We should also close the gate to have a secure place to come back to, just in case we do need to come back." Freya had a point. We can't trust that there was a place to go to in Nashville.

Jana and I agreed with her. I went into Jason's camper to sleep, not only to keep an eye on him, but also because I had never found a camper of my own since we stopped. There wasn't a RV place, but there were some nice vehicles around. I ended up finding myself a nice little Ford Ranger. I think it was a 2020 or newer. It only had ten thousand miles on it! The nice thing was, Freya felt safe enough to drive it, so she would drive my truck while I drove Jason's so he could rest and heal.

Jana went to Stacy's camper and knocked. Stacy called from inside, "Yeah?"

Jana looked over at me and Freya with an odd look on her face, "We are bedding down for the night and will take off first thing in the morning." She waited a few seconds for a reply. "You good, mate?"

Stacy responded finally, without opening the door. "Oh yeah! Sounds great! I'm exhausted."

"Ok, it's settled then." Jana turned to me and Freya with raised eyebrows and walked to her camper. Freya followed her.

I went inside the camper, checked on Jason, who was passed out on his bed, and went to the table and began to turn it into my sleeping area. As I disassembled the table and reassembled it into the bed, I reminded myself that before we left tomorrow, we needed to check the pharmacy in the store for antibiotics and pain meds. We had a few left but not enough for this ride. I lay down and fell asleep as soon as my head hit the pillow.

19.

Justyn was so proud of himself. He was able to find the group, bring a horde to them, kill at least two of them, and then make an escape while they were busy. He fell back just far enough that he could watch them and as far as he could tell, no one was able to see him. The group was hurt, badly. Justyn was proud of himself that he was able to hurt them single-handedly. Sitting in the driver seat of his truck watching the group clean up after the horde attacked them while they were leaving their cozy compound, he wore a huge smile across his face and leaned back, waiting for an idea to come to him. How could he make their lives more miserable? He was the cat and they were the mice he was taunting before the kill.

Justyn woke after a short nap in the cab of his truck. He saw that the group of murderers were still waiting in the same spot he had left them next to the Royerson Supermarket. He was glad he didn't miss them leaving. Justyn adjusted his position in the cab to keep from getting a cramp and said out loud to himself, "Now would be the perfect time to strike. I could set their shit on fire." He was looking at the bottle of lighter fluid he had taken from the store where the group was waiting. He had planned to set fire to the street so they would either be stuck in the little contained village they made or they would roll out and be burned alive. Realizing that wouldn't work, he changed his mind at the last minute when he remembered the small group of townspeople who were now walkers wandering around the bar he had broken into. At that moment, he came up with the plan to lead that small horde over to the area. When Justyn got there, the gate was open and he had just enough time to distract the walkers to hide them and let the group ring the proverbial dinner bell when they rolled out of the gated area. Saved him from having to keep quiet while trying to break into the makeshift gated community and keep himself from becoming zombie food. He had to admit, the plan sucked in the first place because he had been drinking and wasn't thinking clearly. Luckily, Justyn had kept the containers of lighter fluid just in case.

"Should I still go over and set their shit on fire?"

He had thought to himself while feeling the hatred burning inside his guts and spreading like wildfire. He sat there imagining the bright yellow and orange flames licking the sides of the campers and vehicles, spreading like the virus The Federation had released in a coordinated effort. He could hear the ghostly screams of the group, locked inside their rolling homes. He sat back in his seat, a smile spread wide across his face. He knew his father would be proud. His father was always proud of him, but it would be a different pride. Justyn would have avenged his brother and that's bigger than any plan that The Federation had in store for the world. Fuck that stupid organization.

They were, in a way, just as responsible for his brother's death as this group. As Justyn was thinking about The Federation and the group, the sun began peeking over the horizon, washing him in a twilight blue. He was in an even worse mood knowing that he had missed his chance to use them as bonfire kindling. He decided to set them all on fire when they stopped for the night again. For the moment, he would have to play *sneaky squirrel* and follow the group the best he could. That would be difficult in a world where traffic was no longer an issue. He would have to drive far enough behind that they wouldn't see him but not so far that he would miss them if they took a turn. As he was read Justyn g in his seat, he saw a tall lanky kid come out of a camper and walk over to another.

"Good thing I stayed here," he had said quietly to himself. He realized he would have been caught before the flames would have been able to engulf the campers. The last thing he needed was to be caught by these assholes that killed his brother. They would probably kill him, too! That was the last thing his family needed at the moment. He needed to be smart about this. There was only him against maybe five of them now. He had no clue how many there were. Four for sure and a dog. He was not sure if more people were hiding in those rolling coffins. He didn't care. As long as he didn't have to take them all on, face-to-face, and he could sneak around and extinguish their lives, he would win.

20.

Jason woke up moaning and in pain, which in turn woke me up. I can't stand to hear a grown man whine and Jason was doing just that. I looked for some pain meds in his medicine cabinet and then in his bag he always carried but I couldn't find any.

"Jason, I'm gonna have to go see if anyone else has some meds. You don't have any."

"Just be careful," Jason said to me. I'm sure it was killing him that he was hurt. He wasn't much help to the group in his condition and he hated being a burden.

The sun was just breaking over the horizon as I walked out, with my trusty crowbar, of course, to go down the row and ask if anyone had any meds. Jana's camper was first and so I sauntered up to her door and knocked, keeping my eyes peeled for any walkers we missed yesterday or that decided to meander our way on their relentless search for fresh meat. I heard rustling and some groaning but finally the door opened.

"Ugh, yeah?" Jana had said as she opened the door. The sight of her made me chuckle. Her hair was everywhere and she was only able to have one eye open, the other was tightly shut.

"Do you have any painkillers for Jason? He's in a lot of pain this morning."

"Nope. I'm an addict and they wouldn't have lasted long here. I think I gave Stacy all the meds like that each time we found them. She would have them if there are any left."

"Ok, I'm sorry for waking you."

"Nah, I need to get my arse in gear. Thanks for waking me. Do you need help with Jason?"

"I'm good. Thanks."

Jana closed her door and I turned to talk over to Stacy's camper. As I looked up, I saw that her camper was rocking side to side then would stop. It would then do it again and stop.

"Damn, Stacy! Get it! I didn't think you went that way but hey, you love who you love." I said it sort of under my breath. That's when I heard some strange noises with the rocking motion. All of a sudden, I began to get that *ick* feeling you get in the pit of your stomach when something isn't right but you can't just let it go. Nevertheless, I kept walking toward the camper.

I had gotten to the door; my hair was standing up on the back of my neck and I was sweating even though the weather was beautiful this early in the morning. I reached to knock and the camper began rocking again with eerie sounds coming from it like an animal was trapped in there. 'Is that Valkyrie?' I wondered to myself, keeping silent as I stood right outside the door looking at the camper moving. I don't want to even find out what is making this camper move but I have to. Jason needs meds. So...I knock.

The camper stops moving suddenly. My mouth went as dry as the Sahara Desert and I felt weak. My body is giving me all the signs to turn and run but my will is making me stand in place and wait for someone to open the door. No one comes. Do I knock again or do I try the door?

In true "Aaron" fashion, I make the stupid decision to open the door. I put my hand on the doorknob, the camper is still and eerily quiet. I raised my crowbar as I turned the knob and stood off to the right of the door. I jumped back as I swung the door open and out spilled Freya and Stacy. They didn't see me right away and that felt like an eternity, but then Valkyrie leaped out a few seconds later. Valkyrie stopped quickly, turned, and eyeballed me. There was something not right with the dog. She got really low to the ground and started to growl, and that's when I saw the red smeared all over her muzzle, down her neck, and on her back. Valkyrie's eyes were coated with the same white film I had seen dozens of times. She had turned and she was about to leap at me.

I stood at the ready with my crowbar, waiting for the attack that was sure to come. Valkyrie barked at me viciously, only after that did she charge at me. I swung with all my might at her and the curved end of the crowbar connected with her head, sending painful vibrations up the bar to my hands. I dropped the crowbar but the demon dog didn't get up. I had crushed her skull. Poor Valkyrie, she was such a good girl. I wondered how she got infected.

I bent to pick up the crowbar and saw Freya and Stacy getting up off the ground, slowly and very uncoordinated. 'SHIT!' was all I could think of. I was attempting to stay quiet so the two women, who I hoped were still women, didn't turn around and attack me while I was unable to fight back. If they were what I thought they were, I needed the element of surprise. What the hell happened to them? HOW did this happen? Did Stacy get bitten when Big Bertha was on her? Why didn't we check each other over? We got complacent, that's why. We got cocky, that's also why.

Freya and Stacy were standing with their backs to me, weaving and bobbing like one of them. My eyes wandered over the back of their heads and then down their necks, and that's when I saw the bite on Freya. She had a bite on her left shoulder where her neck met. It was confirmed. Valkyrie and Freya were walkers and Stacy probably was as well. I began to walk backward, keeping my eyes on them. I was doing well making my exit till I almost tripped on a huge rock that came from who knows where. That shuffling sound you make trying not to fall on your face? sounds one hundred times louder in complete silence. That got the attention of Freya and Stacy. They turned slowly to the noise I was making and once they saw me, I was fighting for my life. Stacy and Freya both turned to run but, thankfully, fell over each other. That gave me the head start I needed to book it to Jason's truck.

I was able to recover from my stumble and ran to the truck like I had never run before. I reached the camper door with Freya and Stacy following close but it felt like they were on my heels. I had a hard time opening the door but when I finally got the thing open, I raced inside the camper. The girls gripped the door when I almost had it pulled closed.

The slamming of the door on their fingers that they squeezed into the opening before the latch met did not phase them as it would if they were alive. I had to pull the door to me and try to find my crowbar but I needed both hands. All of a sudden I heard it scrape behind me against the floor. Jason had gotten up after hearing me scramble. I see him carefully step over me to get to an angle where he can use the crowbar to push the fingers off. He had no idea what was going on, he just knew walkers were trying to get inside. When Jason was in position, he saw eyes with the white film, blood dripping from the mouth, and then he saw Stacy's face, her mouth biting the air.

"What the FUCK??!?!" Jason yelled as he was pushing the fingers off the door.

Once he got all the fingers off the door and it was able to close and latch, he dropped the crowbar, eyes wild. He could not believe what he saw.

"Aaron, what the fuck was that?"

"Stacy, Freya, and Valkyrie all turned in the night. I was going to ask for some meds for you, the camper was rocking funny..."

Jana raised us on the radio, "Hey guys, I hear some weird shit going on outside..."

"Yeah," Jason responded, "Um...there is a problem. First, do you have any..."

"No, she doesn't. I checked," I interrupted him.

Jason keyed up again, "Oh, Aaron just told me that you don't have any meds. We need to get to Stacy's camper. Stacy, Freya, and Valkyrie are all infected. I don't know how."

"Aaron close? He and I should go check the camper so we can get the meds but someone can watch the other's back." Jana came back over the radio.

Jason looked at me, I lay on the floor and closed my eyes trying to catch my breath. Jason keyed up, "Yeah, give him a minute. He had a struggle with them and the door and he needs to rest for a few. We also want the girls to forget about the can of human sardines and walk away."

"I have to get ready anyway. I'll wait for your call. Over and out."

Jason stood over me and looked down at me, "Ya good?"

"I should be asking YOU that. I know you and Stacy were getting close for a minute."

"I haven't really seen her so it's not even real to me," Jason said in a way that made me think he was kind of numb about it all. "We have been losing people left and right, I'm not sure I have the emotions for it at the moment. I just want my shoulder to stop hurting me." There it was, real and raw. We have been losing people and none of us with family even knew if our families were still alive. I didn't have a family so it was easy for me to not care. I'm not sure what Jason had, family-wise.

"Ok, ask Jana if she's ready."

"Jana, you read me?" Jason said as I dragged myself off the floor to a sitting position. I didn't want to go out there and have to deal with this situation. It was two of my closest friends that I would have to put down and I am really tired of losing people.

"I read you. Is Aaron ready?"

"Yep. About as ready as he'll ever be."

"Let's make fast work of this so we can get the hell away from here," Jana said.

Here it was, the moment of truth. I did not want to do this at all. I wanted to wake up. I wanted to find out that this was a nightmare and that the two girls were fine. I wanted to wake up in the bed of my small studio apartment and find out I was still two months behind on rent. I wasn't sure if I could do this, and Jason didn't seem to act like this was real. The bangs on the door were from other walkers that found us. So many months of this shit, I just couldn't handle it. I had to. I had no other options. This was our life and death was a major part of it.

I got to my feet and put my hand on the door handle. "Tell her I will come get her." I put my ear to the door to see if I could hear them. The pounding had stopped and the shuffling noise was getting quieter, which meant they were either slowing down or they were moving away from the campers. I looked out the door window. Seeing no one, I turned the knob to the camper door as quietly as I could and smoothly pushed it open to give me a line of sight to Jana's camper. There was nothing in the way.

Breathing heavily, but as quietly as I could, I slowly pushed the door open, further exposing me to the outside. The girls were not within sight. I stepped outside and Jason took the door from there to keep it from slamming. There was a slight breeze that could have meant my death if the door had gotten away from me. The morning air was a bit brisk but was warming up with each minute the sun was shining. I slowly walked toward Jana's camper with my head on a swivel.

The day seemed as if it had forgotten that there was a zombie apocalypse. The birds were chirping and I even saw a squirrel skittering across the street. I made it to Jana's camper and slowly started turning the handle. She swung open the door and came out like her place was on fire. I tried to stay quiet and jump back out of her way. She had the same pipe I had seen her with so many times at the ready to bash in some heads. I put my finger to my lips in a *sshhhh*. Jana calmed herself, realizing she came out a lot faster than she should have. We crept over to Stacy's camper, her door still wide open.

I stepped on the metal step leading up to the entryway and it made the loudest metallic creaking noise that anyone had ever heard. That got the attention of Freya and Stacy from the tree line. They were moving faster than any other walker I had ever seen before, and Jana and I hurried into the camper, slamming the door behind us. Within milliseconds, there were snarls, growls, and banging on the door. They knew we were in here and that was the only way out.

Shit...I'm gonna die in here, aren't I?